Foreword by Gabriel García Márquez
Translated by N. J. Sheerin

My discovery of Juan Rulfo – like that of Kafka – will without doubt be an essential chapter in my memoirs. I had arrived in Mexico on the same day Ernest Hemingway pulled the trigger – the 2nd of June 1961 – and not only had I not read Juan Rulfo's books, I hadn't even heard of him. It was very strange: first of all because in those days I kept up to date with the latest goings on in the literary world, and even more so when it came to Latin American novels; secondly because the first people I got in touch with in Mexico were the writers who worked with Manuel Barbachano Ponce[1] in his Dracula's Castle on the streets of Córdoba, and the editors of the literary magazine *Novedades*, headed up by Fernando Benítez.[2] Naturally, they all knew Juan Rulfo well. Yet it was at least six months before anyone mentioned him to me. Perhaps because Juan Rulfo, contrary to what happens with most great authors, is a writer who is much read but little spoken of.

I lived in an apartment without an elevator on calle Renán in the Anzures neighbourhood of Mexico City with Mercedes and Rodrigo, who was less than two years old at the time. There was a double mattress on the floor of the master bedroom, a crib in the other room, and a kitchen table which doubled as a writing desk in the living room, with two single-seat chairs which were put to whatever use was needed. We had decided to stay in this city which at that time still retained a human scale, with its diaphanous air and deliriously coloured flowers in the avenues, but the immigration authorities didn't seem inclined to share in our happiness. Half our lives were spent in immobile queues, sometimes in the rain, in the penitents' courtyards of the Secretariat of the Interior. In my free hours I wrote notes on Colombian literature which I read out live on air for Radio Universidad, then under the auspices of Max Aub.[3] These notes were so honest that one day the Colombian ambassador phoned the broadcaster to lodge a formal complaint. According to him, mine were not notes *on* Colombian literature, but *against* Colombian literature. Max Aub called me to his office, and that, I thought, was the end of the only means of income I had managed to secure in six months. In fact, precisely the opposite happened.

– I haven't had time to listen to the program – Max Aub told me – but if it's as your ambassador says, then it must be very good.

I was thirty-two years old, had in Colombia an ephemeral journalistic career, had just spent three very useful and difficult years in Paris, and eight months in New York, and wanted to write screenplays in Mexico. The Mexican writing community at that time was similar to Colombia's, and I felt very much at home there. Six years earlier I had published my first novel, *Leaf Storm*, and I had three unpublished books:

JUAN RULFO was born in Mexico in 1917. One of Latin America's most esteemed authors, Rulfo's reputation rests on two slim books, his novel *Pedro Páramo* (1955), and *El Llano en llamas* (1953), a collection of short stories, published as *The Burning Plain and Other Stories*. From 1933 Rulfo lived in Mexico City. He obtained a fellowship at the Centro Mexicano de Escritores (Centre for Mexican Authors), which enabled him to write the two books that would make him famous. He later became director of the editorial department of the National Institute for Indigenous Studies. He died in 1986.

JUAN RULFO
PEDRO PÁRAMO

FOREWORD BY **GABRIEL GARCÍA MÁRQUEZ**

Translated by Margaret Sayers Peden

Afterword by Susan Sontag

A complete catalogue record for this book can
be obtained from the British Library on request

The right of Juan Rulfo to be identified as the author of this work has been asserted in
accordance with the Copyright, Designs and Patents Act 1988

Copyright © 1987 by Fondo de Cultura Económica

English translation copyright © 1993 by Northwestern University Press
Foreword copyright © 1980 Gabriel García Márquez
English translation of Foreword copyright © 2014 N. J. Sheerin
Afterword copyright © 1993 Susan Sontag

First published in 1987 in Obras, Fondo de Cultura Económica

First published in the UK in this edition in 2014 by Serpent's Tail
First published in the UK in 1994 by Serpent's Tail
an imprint of Profile Books Ltd
3A Exmouth House
Pine Street
London EC1R 0JH
www.serpentstail.com

ISBN 978 1 78125 316 8

Designed and typeset in Garamond by MacGuru Ltd
info@macguru.org.uk

Printed by CPI Group (UK) Ltd, Croydon CR0 4YY

1 3 5 7 9 10 8 6 4 2

No One Writes to the Colonel, which appeared around that time in Colombia; *In Evil Hour*, which was published by the publishing house Editorial Era shortly afterwards on the recommendation of Vicente Rojo,[4] and the story collection *Big Mama's Funeral*. Of this last I had only incomplete drafts, since Álvaro Mutis[5] had lent the originals to our much-loved Elena Poniatowska[6] before my arrival in Mexico, and she had lost them. Later I managed to reconstruct the stories, and Sergio Galindo[7] published them at the University of Veracruz on the recommendation of Álvaro Mutis.

So I was already a writer with five underground books. For me that wasn't a problem, since neither then nor ever have I written for fame, but rather so that my friends would love me more, and I believed I had managed that. My great problem as a novelist was that after those books I felt I had driven myself up a blind alley, and I was looking everywhere for an escape route. I was well acquainted with good authors and bad authors alike who could have shown me the way out, and yet I felt myself going around and around in concentric circles. I didn't see myself as spent. On the contrary: I felt I still had many novels in me, but I couldn't conceive of a convincing and poetic way of writing them. That is where I was when Álvaro Mutis climbed with great strides the seven storeys up to my apartment with a bundle of books, extracted from this mountain the smallest and shortest, and said as he laughed himself to death:

– Read this shit and learn!

The book was *Pedro Páramo*.

That night I couldn't sleep until I had read it twice. Not since the awesome night I read Kafka's *Metamorphosis* in a down-at-the-heels student boarding house in Bogotá – almost ten years earlier – had I been so overcome. The next day I read *The Plain in Flames*, and my astonishment remained intact. Much later, in a doctor's waiting room, I came across a medical journal with another of Rulfo's scattered masterpieces: 'The Legacy of Matilde Arcángel'. The rest of that year I couldn't read a single other author, because they all seemed inferior.

I still hadn't escaped my bedazzlement when someone told Carlos Velo that I could recite from memory whole passages of *Pedro Páramo*. The truth went even further: I could recite the entire book front to back and vice-versa without a single appreciable error, I could tell you on which page of my edition each scene could be found, and there wasn't a single aspect of its characters' personalities which I wasn't deeply familiar with.

Carlos Velo entrusted me with the adaptation for cinema of another of Juan Rulfo's stories, the only one which I hadn't yet read: 'The Golden Cockerel'. There were sixteen pages of it, very crumpled, typed on disintegrating tissue paper by three different typewriters. Even if they hadn't told me who it was by, I would have known straight away. The language wasn't as intricate as the rest of Juan Rulfo's work, and there were very few of his usual literary devices on show, but his guardian angel flew about every aspect of the writing. Later, Carlos Velo and Carlos Fuentes asked me to read and critique their screenplay for a film adaptation – the first – of *Pedro Páramo*.

I mention these two jobs – the results of which were a long way from being any good – because they obliged me to dive even further into a novel which without doubt I knew better than even its own author (who, by the by, I didn't meet until several years later). Carlos Velo had done something striking: he had cut up the temporal fragments of *Pedro Páramo*, and had reassembled the plot in strictly chronological order. As a straightforward resource to work from it seemed legitimate, although the resulting text was vastly different from the original: flat and disjointed. But it was a useful exercise for me in understanding Juan Rulfo's secret carpentry, and very revealing of his rare wisdom.

There were two fundamental problems with adapting *Pedro Páramo* for screen. The first was the question of names. As subjective as it sounds, in some way every name resembles the person who bears it, and this is something that is much more obvious in fiction than in real life. Juan Rulfo has said – or is claimed to have said – that he takes his characters' names from the headstones of the graves in the cemetery at Jalisco. The only thing we can be certain of is that there are no proper nouns as proper – which is to say, as appropriate – as those borne by the characters in his books. It seemed impossible to me – indeed, it still seems impossible – that an actor could ever be found who would perfectly suit the name of the character he was to play.

The other problem – inseparable from the first – was that of age. Throughout his work, Juan Rulfo has been careful to take very little care with the lifespans of his creations. The critic Narciso Costa Ros recently made a fascinating attempt to establish them in *Pedro Páramo*. I had always thought, purely through poetic intuition, that when Pedro Páramo finally takes Susana San Juan to the Media Luna, his vast domain, she is already sixty-two years old. Pedro Páramo must be around five years her senior. In fact, the whole tragedy seems much greater, much more terrible and beautiful, if the precipitous passion that sets it in motion is so geriatric as to offer no real relief. Such a great and poetic feat would be unthinkable in the cinema. In those darkened theatres, the love lives of the elderly don't move anyone.

The difficult thing about looking at things in this lovely, deliberate way is that poetic sense does not always tally with common sense. The month in which certain scenes occur is essential in any analysis of Juan Rulfo's work, something I doubt he was even conscious of. In poetic works – and *Pedro Páramo* is a poetic work of the highest order – authors often invoke the months of the year for reasons outside strict chronology. What's more: in many cases an author may change the name of the month, day or even year solely to avoid an infelicitous rhyme, or some disharmony, without recognising that these changes can cause a critic to reach an insurmountable conclusion about the work in question. This is the case not just with days and months, but with flowers too. There are writers who use them purely for the sophistication of their names, without paying much attention to whether they correspond to the place or season. This is why it is not uncommon to find books where geraniums flower on the beach and tulips in the snow. In *Pedro Páramo*, where it is impossible to be entirely sure where the line between the living and the dead is drawn, any precision is all the more unattainable. No one can know, of course, how many years death may last.

I wanted to write all this to say that my profound exploration of Juan Rulfo's work was what finally showed me the way to continue with my writing, and for that reason it would be impossible for me to write about him without it seeming that I'm writing about myself. I also want to say that I read it all again before writing these brief reminiscences, and that once again I am the helpless victim of the same astonishment that struck me the first time around. They number scarcely more than three hundred pages, but they are as great – and, I believe, as enduring – as those of Sophocles.

Notes

1. Manuel Barbachano Ponce (1925–1994): A highly influential Mexican producer, most notably of Luís Buñuel's *Nazarín*, he was also a director and screenwriter in his own right. Five years after García Márquez's arrival in Mexico, Barbachano Ponce would co-write the screenplay for Carlos Velo's film adaptation of *Pedro Páramo*.

2. Fernando Benítez Gutiérrez (1912–2000): Widely admired Mexican writer, editor and anthropologist. A champion of Mexico's indigenous population, he is best remembered for his four-volume work *Los Indios de México* (*Indians of Mexico*). Benítez was also famously generous and gave early advice to writers such as Elena Poniatowska, Carlos Monsivais and Jose Emilio Pacheco.

3. Max Aub Mohrenwitz (1903–1972): Spanish-Mexican writer who lived in Mexico in exile from Franco's Spain. A friend of André Malraux, he is most famous for the cycle of novels 'El Labirinto Mágico', set during the Spanish Civil War.

4. Vicente Rojo Almazán (1932–): Barcelona-born Spanish-Mexican artist and member of Mexico's so-called 'Generación de la ruptura' ('Breakaway Generation'), he co-founded Editorial Era and would design the original cover to *One Hundred Years of Solitude.*

5. Álvaro Mutis Jaramillo (1923–2013): Colombian poet, novelist and essayist, and winner of the 2002 Neustadt Prize for Literature, his most famous work in English remains *The Adventures and Misadventures of Maqroll.* He was a close friend of García Márquez, who called him 'one of the greatest writers of our time'.

6. Elena Poniatowska (1932–): French-Mexican novelist and journalist, and winner of the 2013 Cervantes Prize. Her works in English include *Massacre in Mexico*, an investigation into the 1968 Tlatelolco massacre, and *Leonora,* a biography of British-Mexican artist Leonora Carrington, soon to be published in translation by Serpent's Tail.

7. Sergio Galindo Márquez (1926–1993): Mexican novelist and short-story writer, erstwhile director of the Mexican Institute for Fine Arts, member of the Spanish Royal Academy and honorary OBE.

I came to Comala because I had been told that my father, a man named Pedro Páramo, lived there. It was my mother who told me. And I had promised her that after she died I would go see him. I squeezed her hands as a sign I would do it. She was near death, and I would have promised her anything. 'Don't fail to go see him,' she had insisted. 'Some call him one thing, some another. I'm sure he will want to know you.' At the time all I could do was tell her I would do what she asked, and from promising so often I kept repeating the promise even after I had pulled my hands free of her death grip.

Still earlier she had told me:

'Don't ask him for anything. Just what's ours. What he should have given me but never did ... Make him pay, son, for all those years he put us out of his mind.'

'I will, Mother.'

I never meant to keep my promise. But before I knew it my head began to swim with dreams and my imagination took flight. Little by little I began to build a world around a hope centred on the man called Pedro Páramo, the man who had been my mother's husband. That was why I had come to Comala.

It was during the dog days, the season when the August wind blows hot, venomous with the rotten stench of saponaria blossoms.

The road rose and fell. '*It rises or falls depending on whether you're coming or going. If you are leaving, it's uphill; but as you arrive it's downhill.*'

'What did you say that town down there is called?'

'Comala, señor.'

'You're sure that's Comala?'

'I'm sure, señor.'

'It's a sorry-looking place, what happened to it?'

'It's the times, señor.'

I had expected to see the town of my mother's memories, of her nostalgia – nostalgia laced with sighs. She had lived her lifetime sighing about Comala, about going back. But she never had. Now I had come in her place. I was seeing things through her eyes, as she had seen them. She had given me her eyes to see. '*Just as you pass the gate of Los Colimotes there's a beautiful view of a green plain tinged with the yellow of ripe corn. From there you can see Comala, turning the earth white, and lighting it at night.*' Her voice was secret, muffled, as if she were talking to herself ... Mother.

'And why are you going to Comala, if you don't mind my asking?' I heard the man say.

'I've come to see my father,' I replied.

'Umh!' he said.

And again silence.

We were making our way down the hill to the clip-clop of the burros' hooves. Their sleepy eyes were bulging from the August heat.

'You're going to get some welcome.' Again I heard the

voice of the man walking at my side. 'They'll be happy to see someone after all the years no one's come this way.'

After a while he added: 'Whoever you are, they'll be glad to see you.'

In the shimmering sunlight the plain was a transparent lake dissolving in mists that veiled a grey horizon. Farther in the distance, a range of mountains. And farther still, faint remoteness.

'And what does your father look like, if you don't mind my asking?'

'I never knew him,' I told the man. 'I only know his name is Pedro Páramo.'

'Umh! that so?'

'Yes. At least that was the name I was told.'

Yet again I heard the burro driver's 'Umh!'

I had run into him at the crossroads called Los Encuentros. I had been waiting there, and finally this man had appeared.

'Where are you going?' I asked.

'Down thataway, señor.'

'Do you know a place called Comala?'

'That's the very way I'm going.'

So I followed him. I walked along behind, trying to keep up with him, until he seemed to remember I was following and slowed down a little. After that, we walked side by side, so close our shoulders were nearly touching.

'Pedro Páramo's my father, too,' he said.

A flock of crows swept across the empty sky, shrilling 'caw, caw, caw.'

Up- and downhill we went, but always descending. We had left the hot wind behind and were sinking into pure, airless heat. The stillness seemed to be waiting for something.

'It's hot here,' I said.

'You might say. But this is nothing,' my companion replied. 'Try to take it easy. You'll feel it even more when we get to Comala. That town sits on the coals of the earth, at the very mouth of hell. They say that when people from there die and go to hell, they come back for a blanket.'

'Do you know Pedro Páramo?' I asked.

I felt I could ask because I had seen a glimmer of goodwill in his eyes.

'Who is he?' I pressed him.

'Living bile,' was his reply.

And he lowered his stick against the burros for no reason at all, because they had been far ahead of us, guided by the descending trail.

The picture of my mother I was carrying in my pocket felt hot against my heart, as if she herself were sweating. It was an old photograph, worn around the edges, but it was the only one I had ever seen of her. I had found it in the kitchen safe, inside a clay pot filled with herbs: dried lemon balm, castilla blossoms, sprigs of rue. I had kept it with me ever since. It was all I had. My mother always hated having her picture taken. She said photographs were a tool of witchcraft. And that may have been so, because hers was riddled with pinpricks, and at the location of the heart there was a hole you could stick your middle finger through.

I had brought the photograph with me, thinking it might help my father recognize who I was.

'Take a look,' the burro driver said, stopping. 'You see that rounded hill that looks like a hog bladder? Well, the Media Luna lies right behind there. Now turn thataway. You see the brow of that hill? Look hard. And now back this way. You see that ridge? The one so far you can't hardly see it? Well, all that's the Media Luna. From end to end. Like they say, as far as the eye can see. He owns ever' bit of that land. We're Pedro Páramo's sons, all right, but, for all that, our mothers brought us into the world on straw mats. And the real joke of it is that he's the one carried us to be baptized. That's how it was with you, wasn't it?'

'I don't remember.'

'The hell you say!'

'What did you say?'

'I said, we're getting there, señor.'

'Yes. I see it now ... What could it have been?'

'That was a *correcaminos*, señor. A roadrunner. That's what they call those birds around here.'

'No. I meant I wonder what could have happened to the town? It looks so deserted, abandoned really. In fact, it looks like no one lives here at all.'

'It doesn't just look like no one lives here. No one does live here.'

'And Pedro Páramo?'

'Pedro Páramo died years ago.'

It was the hour of the day when in every little village children come out to play in the streets, filling the afternoon with their cries. The time when dark walls still reflect pale yellow sunlight.

At least that was what I had seen in Sayula, just yesterday at this hour. I'd seen the still air shattered by the flight of doves flapping their wings as if pulling themselves free of the day. They swooped and plummeted above the tile rooftops, while the children's screams whirled and seemed to turn blue in the dusk sky.

Now here I was in this hushed town. I could hear my footsteps on the cobbled paving stones. Hollow footsteps, echoing against walls stained red by the setting sun.

This was the hour I found myself walking down the main street. Nothing but abandoned houses, their empty doorways overgrown with weeds. What had the stranger told me they were called? '*La gobernadora*, señor. Creosote bush. A plague that takes over a person's house the minute he leaves. You'll see.'

As I passed a street corner, I saw a woman wrapped in her rebozo; she disappeared as if she had never existed. I started forward again, peering into the doorless houses. Again the woman in the rebozo crossed in front of me.

'Evening,' she said.

I looked after her. I shouted: 'Where will I find doña Eduviges?'

She pointed: 'There. The house beside the bridge.'

I took note that her voice had human overtones, that her

mouth was filled with teeth and a tongue that worked as she spoke, and that her eyes were the eyes of people who inhabit the earth.

By now it was dark.

She turned to call good night. And though there were no children playing, no doves, no blue-shadowed roof tiles, I felt that the town was alive. And that if I heard only silence, it was because I was not yet accustomed to silence – maybe because my head was still filled with sounds and voices.

Yes, voices. And here, where the air was so rare, I heard them even stronger. They lay heavy inside me. I remembered what my mother had said: '*You will hear me better there. I will be closer to you. You will hear the voice of my memories stronger than the voice of my death – that is, if death ever had a voice.*' Mother ... So alive.

How I wished she were here, so I could say, 'You were mistaken about the house. You told me the wrong place. You sent me "south of nowhere," to an abandoned village. Looking for someone who's no longer alive.'

I found the house by the bridge by following the sound of the river. I lifted my hand to knock, but there was nothing there. My hand met only empty space, as if the wind had blown open the door. A woman stood there. She said, 'Come in.' And I went in.

So I stayed in Comala. The man with the burros had gone on his way. Before leaving, he'd said:

'I still have a way to go, yonder where you see that band of hills. My house is there. If you want to come, you will be welcome. For now, if you want to stay here, then stay. You got nothing to lose by taking a look around, you may find someone who's still among the living.'

I stayed. That was why I had come.

'Where can I find lodging?' I called, almost shouting now.

'Look up doña Eduviges, if she's still alive. Tell her I sent you.'

'And what's your name?'

' Abundio,' he called back. But he was too far for me to hear his last name.

'I am Eduviges Dyada. Come in.'

It was as if she had been waiting for me. Everything was ready, she said, motioning for me to follow her through a long series of dark, seemingly empty, rooms. But no. As soon as my eyes grew used to the darkness and the thin thread of light following us, I saw shadows looming on either side, and sensed that we were walking down a narrow passageway opened between bulky shapes.

'What do you have here?' I asked.

'Odds and ends,' she said. 'My house is chock full of other people's things. As people went away, they chose my house to store their belongings, but not one of them has ever come back to claim them. The room I kept for you is here at the back. I keep it cleaned out in case anyone comes. So you're her son?'

'Whose son?' I asked.

'Doloritas's boy.'

'Yes. But how did you know?'

'She told me you would be coming. Today, in fact. That you would be coming today.'

'Who told you? My mother?'

'Yes. Your mother.'

I did not know what to think. But Eduviges left me no time for thinking.

'This is your room,' she said.

The room had no doors, except for the one we had entered. She lighted the candle, and I could see the room was completely empty.

'There's no place to sleep,' I said.

'Don't worry about that. You must be tired from your journey, and weariness makes a good mattress. I'll fix you up a bed first thing in the morning. You can't expect me to have things ready on the spur of the moment. A person needs some warning, and I didn't get word from your mother until just now.'

'My mother?' I said. 'My mother is dead.'

'So that was why her voice sounded so weak, like it had to travel a long distance to get here. Now I understand. And when did she die?'

'A week ago.'

'Poor woman. She must of thought I'd forsaken her. We made each other a promise we'd die together. That we would go hand in hand, to lend each other courage on our last journey – in case we had need for something, or ran into trouble. We were the best of friends. Didn't she ever talk about me?'

'No, never.'

'That's strange. Of course, we were just girls then. She was barely married. But we loved each other very much. Your mother was so pretty, so, well, sweet, that it made a person happy to love her. You wanted to love her. So, she got a head start on me, eh? Well, you can be sure I'll catch up with her. No one knows better than I do how far heaven is, but I also know all the shortcuts. The secret is to die, God willing, when you want to, and not when He proposes. Or else to force Him to take you before your time. Forgive me for going on like this, talking to you as if we were old friends, but I do it because you're like my own son. Yes, I said it a thousand times: "Dolores's boy should have been my son." I'll tell you why sometime. All I want to say now is that I'll catch up with your mother along one of the roads to eternity.'

I wondered if she were crazy. But by now I wasn't thinking at all. I felt I was in a faraway world and let myself be pulled along by the current. My body, which felt weaker and weaker, surrendered completely; it had slipped its ties and anyone who wanted could have wrung me out like a rag.

'I'm tired,' I said.

'Come eat something before you sleep. A bite. Anything there is.'

'I will. I'll come later.'

Water dripping from the roof tiles was forming a hole in the sand of the patio. Plink! plink! and then another plink! as drops struck a bobbing, dancing laurel leaf caught in a crack between the adobe bricks. The storm had passed. Now an intermittent breeze shook the branches of the pomegranate tree, loosing showers of heavy rain, spattering the ground with gleaming drops that dulled as they sank into the earth. The hens, still huddled on their roost, suddenly flapped their wings and strutted out to the patio, heads bobbing, pecking worms unearthed by the rain. As the clouds retreated the sun flashed on the rocks, spread an iridescent sheen, sucked water from the soil, shone on sparkling leaves stirred by the breeze.

'What's taking you so long in the privy, son?'

'Nothing, mamá.'

'If you stay in there much longer, a snake will come and bite you.'

'Yes, mamá.'

I was thinking of you, Susana. Of the green hills. Of when we used to fly kites in the windy season. We could hear the sounds of life from the town below; we were high above on the hill, playing out string to the wind. 'Help me, Susana.' And soft hands would tighten on mine. 'Let out more string.'

The wind made us laugh; our eyes followed the string running through our fingers after the wind until with a faint pop! it broke, as if it had been snapped by the wings of a bird. And high overhead, the paper bird would tumble and somersault, trailing its rag tail, until it disappeared into the green earth.

Your lips were moist, as if kissed by the dew.

'I told you, son, come out of the privy now.'

'Yes, mamá. I'm coming.'

I was thinking of you. Of the times you were there looking at me with your aquamarine eyes.

He looked up and saw his mother in the doorway.

'What's taking you so long? What are you doing in there?'

'I'm thinking.'

'Can't you do it somewhere else? It's not good for you to stay in the privy so long. Besides, you should be doing something. Why don't you go help your grandmother shell corn?'

'I'm going, mamá. I'm going.'

Grandmother, I've come to help you shell corn.'

'We're through with that, but we still have to grind the chocolate. Where have you been? We were looking for you all during the storm.'

'I was in the back patio.'

'And what were you doing? Praying?'

'No, Grandmother. I was just watching it rain.'

His grandmother looked at him with those yellow-grey eyes that seemed to see right through a person.

'Run clean the mill, then.'

Hundreds of meters above the clouds, far, far above everything, you are hiding, Susana. Hiding in God's immensity, behind His Divine Providence where I cannot touch you or see you, and where my words cannot reach you.

'Grandmother, the mill's no good. The grinder's broken.'

'That Micaela must have run corn through it. I can't break her of that habit, but it's too late now.'

'Why don't we buy a new one? This one's so old it isn't any good anyway.'

'That's the Lord's truth. But with all the money we spent to bury your grandfather, and the tithes we've paid to the church, we don't have anything left. Oh, well, we'll do without something else and buy a new one. Why don't you run see doña Inés Villalpando and ask her to carry us on her books until October. We'll pay her at harvest time.'

'All right, Grandmother.'

'And while you're at it, to kill two birds with one stone, ask her to lend us a sifter and some clippers. The way those weeds are growing, we'll soon have them growing out our ears. If I had my big house with all my stock pens, I wouldn't be complaining. But your grandfather took care of that when he moved here. Well, it must be God's will. Things seldom work out the way you want. Tell doña Inés that after harvest time we'll pay her everything we owe her.'

'Yes, Grandmother.'

Hummingbirds. It was the season. He heard the whirring of their wings in blossom-heavy jasmine.

He stopped by the shelf where the picture of the Sacred Heart stood, and found twenty-four centavos. He left the four single coins and took the veinte.

As he was leaving, his mother stopped him:

'Where are you going?'

'Down to doña Inés Villalpando's, to buy a new mill. Ours broke.'

'Ask her to give you a meter of black taffeta, like this,' and she handed him a piece. 'And to put it on our account.'

'All right, mamá.'

'And on the way back, buy me some aspirin. You'll find some money in the flowerpot in the hall.'

He found a peso. He left the veinte and took the larger coin. 'Now I have enough money for anything that comes along,' he thought.

'Pedro!' people called to him. 'Hey, Pedro!'

But he did not hear. He was far, far away.

During the night it began to rain again. For a long time, he lay listening to the gurgling of the water; then he must have slept, because when he awoke, he heard only a quiet drizzle. The windowpanes were misted over and raindrops were threading down like tears ... I watched the trickles glinting in the lightning flashes, and every breath I breathed, I sighed. And every thought I thought was of you, Susana.

The rain turned to wind. He heard '... the forgiveness of sins and the resurrection of the flesh. Amen.' That was deeper in the house, where women were telling the last of their beads. They got up from their prayers, they penned up the chickens, they bolted the door, they turned out the light.

Now there was only the light of night, and rain hissing like the murmur of crickets.

'Why didn't you come say your Rosary? We were making a novena for your grandfather.'

His mother was standing in the doorway, candle in hand. Her long, crooked shadow stretched toward the ceiling. The roof beams repeated it, in fragments.

'I feel sad,' he said.

Then she turned away. She snuffed out the candle. As she closed the door, her sobs began; he could hear them for a long time, mixed with the sound of the rain.

The church clock tolled the hours, hour after hour, hour after hour, as if time had been telescoped.

'Oh, yes. I was nearly your mother. She never told you anything about it?'

'No. She only told me good things. I heard about you from the man with the train of burros. The man who led me here, the one named Abundio.'

'He's a good man, Abundio. So, he still remembers me? I used to give him a little something for every traveller he sent to my house. It was a good deal for both of us. Now, sad to say, times have changed, and since the town has fallen on bad times, no one brings us any news. So he told you to come see me?'

'Yes, he said to look for you.'

'I'm grateful to him for that. He was a good man, one you could trust. It was him that brought the mail, and he kept right on even after he went deaf. I remember the black day it happened. Everyone felt bad about it, because we all liked him. He brought letters to us and took ours away. He always told us how things were going on the other side of the world, and doubtless he told them how we were making out. He was a big talker. Well, not afterward. He stopped talking then. He said there wasn't much point in saying things he couldn't hear, things that evaporated in the air, things he couldn't get the taste of. It all happened when one of those big rockets we use to scare off water snakes went off too close to his head. From that day on, he never spoke, though he wasn't struck dumb. But one thing I tell you, it didn't make him any less a good person.'

'The man I'm talking about heard fine.'

'Then it can't have been him. Besides, Abundio died. I'm sure he's dead. So you see? It couldn't have been him.'

'I guess you're right.'

'Well, getting back to your mother. As I was telling you ...'

As I listened to her drone on, I studied the woman before me. I thought she must have gone through some bad times. Her face was transparent, as if the blood had drained from it, and her hands were all shrivelled, nothing but wrinkled claws. Her eyes were sunk out of sight. She was wearing an old-fashioned white dress with rows of ruffles, and around her neck, strung on a cord, she wore a medal of the María Santísima del Refugio with the words 'Refuge of Sinners.'

'... This man I'm telling you about broke horses over at the Media Luna ranch; he said his name was Inocencio Osorio. Everyone knew him, though, by his nickname 'Cockleburr'; he could stick to a horse like a burr to a blanket. My compadre Pedro used to say that the man was born to break colts. The fact is, though, that he had another calling: conjuring. He conjured up dreams. That was who he really was. And he put it over on your mother, like he did so many others. Including me. Once when I was feeling bad, he showed up and said, 'I've come to give you a treatment so's you'll feel better.' And what that meant was he would start out kneading and rubbing you: first your fingertips, then he'd stroke your hands, then your arms. First thing you knew he'd be working on your legs, rubbing hard, and soon you'd be feeling warm all over. And all the time he was rubbing and stroking he'd be telling you your fortune. He would fall into a trance and roll his eyes and conjure and curse, with spittle flying everywhere – you'd of thought he was a gypsy. Sometimes he would end up stark naked; he said we wanted it that way. And sometimes what he said came true. He shot at so many targets that once in a while he was bound to hit one.

'So what happened was that when your mother went to see this Osorio, he told her that she shouldn't lie with a man that night because the moon was wrong.

'Dolores came and told me everything, in a quandary about what to do. She said there was no two ways about it, she couldn't go to bed with Pedro Páramo that night. Her wedding night. And there I was, trying to convince her she shouldn't put any stock in that Osorio, who was nothing but a swindler and a liar.

'"I *can't*," she told me. "You go for me. He'll never catch on."

'Of course I was a lot younger than she was. And not quite as dark-skinned. But you can't tell that in the dark.

'"It'll never work, Dolores. You have to go."

'"Do me this one favour, and I'll pay you back a hundred times over."

'In those days your mother had the shyest eyes. If there was something pretty about your mother, it was those eyes. They could really win you over.

'"You go in my place," she kept saying.

'So I went.

'I took courage from the darkness, and from something else your mother didn't know, and that was that she wasn't the only one who liked Pedro Páramo.

'I crawled in bed with him. I was happy to; I wanted to. I cuddled right up against him, but all the celebrating had worn him out and he spent the whole night snoring. All he did was wedge his legs between mine.

'Before dawn, I got up and went to Dolores. I said to her: "You go now. It's a new day."

'"What did he do to you?" she asked me.

'"I'm still not sure," I told her.

'You were born the next year, but I wasn't your mother, though you came within a hair of being mine.

'Maybe your mother was ashamed to tell you about it.'

Green pastures. Watching the horizon rise and fall as the wind swirled through the wheat, an afternoon rippling with curling lines of rain. The colour of the earth, the smell of alfalfa and bread. A town that smelled like spilled honey ...

'She always hated Pedro Páramo. "Doloritas! Did you tell them to get my breakfast?" Your mother was up every morning before dawn. She would start the fire from the coals, and with the smell of the tinder the cats would wake up. Back and forth through the house, followed by her guard of cats. "Doña Doloritas!"

'I wonder how many times your mother heard that call? "Doña Doloritas, this is cold. It won't do." How many times? And even though she was used to the worst of times, those shy eyes of hers grew hard.'

Not to know any taste but the savour of orange blossoms in the warmth of summer.

'Then she began her sighing.

'"Why are you sighing so, Doloritas?"

'I had gone with them that afternoon. We were in the middle of a field, watching the bevies of young thrushes. One solitary buzzard rocked lazily in the sky.

'"Why are you sighing, Doloritas?"

'"I wish I were a buzzard so I could fly to where my sister lives."

'"That's the last straw, doña Doloritas! You'll see your sister, all right. Right now. We're going back to the house and you're going to pack your suitcases. That was the last straw!"

'And your mother went. "I'll see you soon, don Pedro."

'"Good-bye, Doloritas!"

'And she never came back to the Media Luna. Some months later, I asked Pedro Páramo about her.

'"She loved her sister more than she did me. I guess she's happy there. Besides, I was getting fed up with her. I have no intention of asking about her, if that's what's worrying you."

'But how will they get along?'

'"Let God look after them."

... Make him pay, Son, for all those years he put us out of his mind.

'And that's how it was until she advised me that you were coming to see me. We never heard from her again.'

'A lot has happened since then,' I told Eduviges. 'We lived in Colima. We were taken in by my Aunt Gertrudis, who threw it in our faces every day that we were a burden. She used to ask my mother, "Why don't you go back to your husband?"

'"Oh? Has he sent for me? I'm not going back unless he asks me to. I came because I wanted to see you. Because I loved you. That's why I came."

'"I know that. But it's time now for you to leave."

'"If it was up to me ..."'

I thought that Eduviges was listening to me. I noticed, though, that her head was tilted as if she were listening to some faraway sound. Then she said:

'When will you rest?'

The day you went away I knew I would never see you again. You were stained red by the late afternoon sun, by the dusk filling the sky with blood. You were smiling. You had often said of the town you were leaving behind, 'I like it because of you; but I hate everything else about it – even having been born here.' I thought, she will never come back; I will never see her again.

'What are you doing here at this hour? Aren't you working?'

'No, Grandmother. Rogelio asked me to mind his little boy. I'm just walking him around. I can't do both things – the kid and the telegraph. Meanwhile he's down at the poolroom drinking beer. On top of everything else, he doesn't pay me anything.'

'You're not there to be paid. You're there to learn. Once you know something, then you can afford to make demands. For now, you're just an apprentice. Maybe one day you will be the boss. But for that you need patience and, above all, humility. If they want you to take the boy for a walk, do it, for heaven's sake. You must learn to be patient.'

'Let others be patient, Grandmother. I'm not one for patience.'

'You and your wild ideas! I'm afraid you have a hard row ahead of you, Pedro Páramo.'

'What was that I just heard, doña Eduviges?'

She shook her head as if waking from a dream.

'That's Miguel Páramo's horse, galloping down the road to the Media Luna.'

'Then someone's living there?'

'No, no one's living there.'

'But ...?'

'It's only his horse, coming and going. They were never apart. It roams the countryside, looking for him, and it's always about this time it comes back. It may be that the poor creature can't live with its remorse. Even animals realize when they've done something bad, don't they?'

'I don't understand. I didn't hear anything that sounded like a horse.'

'No?'

'No.'

'Then it must be my sixth sense. A gift God gave me – or maybe a curse. All I know is that I've suffered because of it.'

She said nothing for a while, but then added:

'It all began with Miguel Páramo. I was the only one knew everything that happened the night he died. I'd already gone to bed when I heard his horse galloping back toward the Media Luna. I was surprised, because Miguel never came home at that hour. It was always early morning before he got back. He went every night to be with his sweetheart over in a town called Contla, a good distance from here. He left early and got back late. But that night he never returned ... You hear it now? Of course you can hear it. It's his horse coming home.'

'I don't hear anything.'

'Then it's just me. Well, like I was saying, the fact that he didn't come back wasn't the whole story. His horse had no more than gone by when I heard someone rapping at my window. Now you be the judge of whether it was my imagination. What I know is that something made me get up and go see who it was. And it was him. Miguel Páramo. I wasn't surprised to see him, because there was once a time when he spent every night at my house, sleeping with me – until he met that girl who drank his blood.

'"What's happened," I asked Miguel Páramo. "Did she give you the gate?"

'"No. She still loves me," he said. "The problem is that I couldn't locate her. I couldn't find my way to the town. There was a lot of mist or smoke or something. I do know that Contla isn't there anymore. I rode right past where it ought to be, according to my calculations, and there was nothing there. I've come to tell you about it, because I know you will understand. If I told anyone else in Comala they'd say I'm crazy – the way they always have."

"'No. Not crazy, Miguel. You must be dead. Remember, everyone told you that horse would be the death of you one day. Remember that, Miguel Páramo. Maybe you did do something crazy, but that's another matter now.'

"'All I did was jump that new stone fence my father had built. I asked El Colorado to jump it so I wouldn't have to go all the way around, the way you have to now to get to the road. I know that I jumped it, and then kept on riding. But like I told you, everything was smoke, smoke, smoke.'

"'Your father's going to be sick with grief in the morning,' I told him. 'I feel sorry for him. Now go, and rest in peace, Miguel. I thank you for coming to say good-bye.'

'And I closed the window. Before dawn, a ranch hand from the Media Luna came to tell me, "The *patrón* is asking for you. Young Miguel is dead. Don Pedro wants your company."

"'I already knew,' I told him. 'Did they tell you to cry?'

"'Yes. Don Fulgor told me to cry when I told you.'

"'All right. You tell don Pedro that I'll be there. How long ago did they bring him back?'

"'No more than half an hour. If it'd been sooner, maybe they could of saved him. Although the doctor who looked him over said he had been cold for some time. We learned about it when El Colorado came home with an empty saddle and made such a stir that no one could sleep. You know how him and that horse loved one another, and as for me, I think the animal is suffering more than don Pedro. He hasn't eaten or slept, and all he does is chase around in circles. Like he knows, you know? Like he feels all broken and chewed up inside."

"'Don't forget to close the door as you go."

'And with that the hand from the Media Luna left.'

'Have you ever heard the moan of a dead man?' she asked me.

'No, doña Eduviges.'

'You're lucky.'

Drops are falling steadily on the stone trough. The air carries the sound of the clear water escaping the stone and falling into the storage urn. He is conscious of sounds: feet scraping the ground, back and forth, back and forth. The endless dripping. The urn overflows, spilling water onto the wet earth.

'Wake up,' someone is saying.

He hears the sound of the voice. He tries to identify it, but he sinks back down and drowses again, crushed by the weight of sleep. Hands tug at the covers; he snuggles beneath their warmth, seeking peace.

'Wake up!' Again someone is calling.

That someone is shaking his shoulders. Making him sit up. He half opens his eyes. Again he hears the dripping of water falling from the stone into the brimming urn. And those shuffling footsteps ... And weeping.

Then he heard the weeping. That was what woke him: a soft but penetrating weeping that because it was so delicate was able to slip through the mesh of sleep and reach the place where his fear lived.

Slowly he got out of bed; he saw a woman's face resting against a door frame still darkened by night. The woman was sobbing.

'Why are you crying, mamá?' he asked; the minute his feet touched the floor he recognized his mother's face.

'Your father is dead,' she said.

And then, as if her coiled grief had suddenly burst free, she turned and turned in a tight circle until hands grasped her shoulders and stopped the spiralling of her tortured body.

Through the door he could see the dawn. There were no stars. Only a leaden grey sky still untouched by the rays of the sun. A drab light that seemed more like the onset of night than the beginning of day.

Outside in the patio, the footsteps, like people wandering in circles. Muted sounds. And inside, the woman standing in the doorway, her body impeding the arrival of day: through her arms he glimpsed pieces of sky and, beneath her feet, trickles of light. A damp light, as if the floor beneath the woman were flooded with tears. And then the sobbing. Again the soft but penetrating weeping, and the grief contorting her body with pain.

'They've killed your father.'

And you, Mother? Who killed you?

'There is wind and sun, and there are clouds. High above, blue sky, and beyond that there may be songs; perhaps sweeter voices ... In a word, hope. There is hope for us, hope to ease our sorrows.

'But not for you, Miguel Páramo, for you died without for-giveness and you will never know God's grace.'

Father Rentería walked around the corpse, reciting the mass for the dead. He hurried in order to finish quickly, and he left without offering the final benediction to the people who filled the church.

'Father, we want you to bless him!'

'No,' he said, shaking his head emphatically. 'I won't give my blessing. He was an evil man, and he shall not enter the Kingdom of Heaven. God will not smile on me if I intercede for him.'

As he spoke, he clasped his hands tightly, hoping to conceal their trembling. To no avail.

That corpse weighed heavily on the soul of everyone present. It lay on a dais in the centre of the church, sur-rounded with new candles and flowers; a father stood there, alone, waiting for the mass to end.

Father Rentería walked past Pedro Páramo, trying not to brush against him. He raised the aspergillum gently, sprink-ling holy water from the top of the coffin to the bottom, while a murmur issued from his lips that might have been a prayer. Then he knelt, and everyone knelt with him:

'Oh, God, have mercy on this Your servant.'

'May he rest in peace, Amen,' the voices chorused.

Then, as his rage was building anew, he saw that everyone was leaving the church, and that they were carrying out the body of Miguel Páramo.

Pedro Páramo approached him and knelt beside him:

'I know you hated him, Father. And with reason. Rumour has it that your brother was murdered by my son, and you believe that your niece Ana was raped by him. Then there were his insults, and his lack of respect. Those are all reasons anyone could understand. But forget all that now, Father. Weigh him and forgive him, as perhaps God has forgiven him.'

He placed a handful of gold coins on the prie-dieu and got to his feet: 'Take this as a gift for your church.'

The church was empty now. Two men stood in the doorway, waiting for Pedro Páramo. He joined them, and together they followed the coffin that had been waiting for them, resting on the shoulders of four foremen from the Media Luna. Father Rentería picked up the coins, one by one, and walked to the altar.

'These are Yours,' he said. 'He can afford to buy salvation. Only you know whether this is the price. As for me, Lord, I throw myself at your feet to ask for the justice or injustice that any of us may ask ... For my part, I hope you damn him to hell.'

And he closed the chapel.

He walked to the sacristy, threw himself into a corner, and sat there weeping with grief and sorrow until his tears were exhausted.

'All right, Lord. You win,' he said.

At suppertime, he drank his hot chocolate as he did every night. He felt calm.

'So, Anita. Do you know who was buried today?'

'No, Uncle.'

'You remember Miguel Páramo?'

'Yes, Uncle.'

'Well, that's who.'

Ana hung her head.

'You *are* sure he was the one, aren't you?'

'I'm not positive, Uncle. No. I never saw his face. He surprised me at night, and it was dark.'

'Then how did you know it was Miguel Páramo?'

'Because he said so: "It's Miguel Páramo, Ana. Don't be afraid." That was what he said.'

'But you knew he was responsible for your father's death, didn't you?'

'Yes, Uncle.'

'So what did you do to make him leave?'

'I didn't do anything.'

The two sat without speaking. They could hear the warm breeze stirring in the myrtle leaves.

'He said that was why he had come: to say he was sorry and to ask me to forgive him. I lay still in my bed, and I told him, "The window is open." And he came in. The first thing he did was put his arms around me, as if that was his way of asking forgiveness for what he had done. And I smiled at him. I remembered what you had taught me: that we must never hate anyone. I smiled to let him know that, but then I realized that he couldn't see my smile because it was so black that I couldn't see him. I could only feel his body on top of me, and feel him beginning to do bad things to me.

'I thought he was going to kill me. That's what I believed, Uncle. Then I stopped thinking at all, so I would be dead before he killed me. But I guess he didn't dare.

'I knew he hadn't when I opened my eyes and saw the morning light shining in the open window. Up till then, I felt that I had in fact died.'

'But you must have some way of being sure. His voice. Didn't you recognize him by his voice?'

'I didn't recognize him at all. All I knew about him was that he had killed my father. I had never seen him, and afterward I never saw him again. I couldn't have faced him, Uncle.'

'But you knew who he was.'

'Yes. And what he was. And I know that by now he must be in the deepest pit of hell. I prayed to all the saints with all my heart and soul.'

'Don't be too sure of that, my child. Who knows how many people are praying for him! You are alone. One prayer against thousands. And among them, some much more intense than yours – like his father's.'

He was about to say: 'And anyway, I have pardoned him.' But he only thought it. He did not want to add hurt to the girl's already broken spirit. Instead, he took her arm and said:

'Let us give thanks to the Lord our God, Who has taken him from this earth where he caused such harm; what does it matter if He lifted him to His heaven?'

A horse galloped by the place where the main street crosses the road to Contla. No one saw it. Nevertheless, a woman waiting on the outskirts of the village told that she had seen the horse, and that its front legs were buckled as if about to roll head over hooves. She recognized it as Miguel Páramo's chestnut stallion. The thought had even crossed her mind that the animal was going to break its neck. Then she saw it regain its footing and without any interruption in stride race off with its head twisted back, as if frightened by something it had left behind.

That story reached the Media Luna on the night of the burial, as the men were resting after the long walk back from the cemetery.

They were talking, as people talk everywhere before turning in.

'That death pained me in more ways than one,' said Terencio Lubianes. 'My shoulders are still sore.'

'Mine, too,' said his brother Ubillado. 'And my bunions must have swelled an inch. All because the *patrón* wanted us to wear shoes. You'd of thought it was a holy day, right, Toribio?'

'What do you want me to say? I think it was none too soon he died.'

In a few days there was more news from Contla. It came with the latest ox cart.

'They're saying that his spirit is wandering over there. They've seen it rapping at the window of a lady friend. It was just like him. Chaps and all.'

'And do you think that don Pedro, with that disposition of his, would allow his son to keep calling on the women? I can just imagine what he'd say if he found out: "All right," he'd say. "You're dead now. You keep to your grave. And leave the affairs to us." And if he caught him wandering around, you can bet he'd put him back in the ground for good.'

'You're right about that, Isaías. That old man doesn't put up with much.'

The driver went on his way. 'I'm just telling you what was told me.'

Shooting stars. They fell as if the sky were raining fire.

'Look at that,' said Terencio. 'Please look at the show they're putting on up there.'

'Must be celebrating Miguelito's arrival,' Jesus put in.

'You don't think it's a bad omen?'

'Bad for who?'

'Maybe your sister's lonesome and wants him back.'

'Who're you talking to?'

'To you.'

'It's time to go, boys. We've travelled a long road today, and we have to be up early tomorrow.'

And they faded into the night like shadows.

Shooting stars. One by one, the lights in Comala went out.

Then the sky took over the night.

Father Rentería tossed and turned in his bed, unable to sleep.

It's all my fault, he told himself. Everything that's happening. Because I'm afraid to offend the people who provide for me. It's true; I owe them my livelihood. I get nothing from the poor, and God knows prayers don't fill a stomach. That's how it's been up to now. And we're seeing the consequences. All my fault. I have betrayed those who love me and who have put their faith in me and come to me to intercede on their behalf with God. What has their faith won them? Heaven? Or the purification of their souls? And why purify their souls anyway, when at the last moment ... I will never forget María Dyada's face when she came to ask me to save her sister Eduviges:

'She always served her fellowmen. She gave them everything she had. She even gave them sons. All of them. And took the infants to their fathers to be recognized. But none of them wanted to. Then she told them, "In that case, I'll be the father as well, even though fate chose me to be the mother." Everyone took advantage of her hospitality and her good nature; she never wanted to offend, or set anyone against her.'

'But she took her own life. She acted against the will of God.'

'She had no choice. That was another thing she did out of the goodness of her heart.'

'"She fell short at the last hour," that's what I told María Dyada. "At the last minute. So many good acts stored up for her salvation, and then to lose them like that, all at once!"'

'But she didn't lose them. She died of her sorrows. And sorrow ... You once told us something about sorrow that I can't remember now. It was because of her sorrows she went away. And died choking on her own blood. I can still see how she looked. That face was the saddest face I have ever seen on a human.'

'Perhaps with many prayers ...'

'We're already saying many prayers, Father.'

'I mean maybe, just perhaps, with Gregorian masses. But for that we would need help, have to bring priests here. And that costs money.'

And there before my eyes was the face of María Dyada, a poor woman still ripe with children.

'I don't have money. You know that, Father.'

'Let's leave things as they are. Let us put our hope in God.'

'Yes, Father.'

Why did she look courageous in her resignation? And what would it have cost him to grant pardon when it was so easy to say a word or two – or a hundred if a hundred were needed to save a soul? What did he know of heaven and hell? And yet even an old priest buried in a nameless town knew who had deserved heaven. He knew the roll. He began to run through the list of saints in the Catholic pantheon, beginning with the saints for each day of the calendar: 'Saint Nunilona, virgin and martyr; Anercio, bishop; Saints Salomé, widow, and Alo-dia-or-Elodia and Nulina, virgins; Córdula and Donate.' And on down the line. He was drifting off to sleep when he sat up straight in his bed. 'Here I am reciting the saints as if I were counting sheep.'

He went outside and looked at the sky. It was raining stars. He was sorry, because he would rather have seen a tranquil sky. He heard roosters crowing. He felt the mantle of night covering the earth. The earth, 'this vale of tears.'

'You're lucky, son. Very lucky,' Eduviges Dyada told me.

It was very late by now. The lamp in the corner was beginning to grow dim; it flickered and went out.

I sensed that the woman rose, and I supposed she was leaving to get another lamp. I listened to her receding footsteps. I sat there, waiting.

After a while, when I realized that she was not coming back, I got up, too. I inched my way forward, groping in the darkness, until I reached my room. I lay down on the floor to wait for sleep to come.

I slept fitfully.

It was during one of those intervals that I heard the cry. It was a drawn-out cry, like the howl of a drunk. 'Ay-y-y-y, life! I am too good for you!'

I sat bolt upright because it had sounded almost in my ear. It could have been in the street, but I had heard it here, sticking to the walls of my room. When I awoke, everything was silent: nothing but the sound of moths working and the murmur of silence.

No, there was no way to judge the depth of the silence that followed that scream. It was as if the earth existed in a vacuum. No sound: not even of my breathing or the beating of my heart. As if the very sound of consciousness had been stilled. And just when the pause ended, and I was regaining my calm, the cry was repeated; I heard it for a long, long while. 'You owe me something, even if it's nothing more than a hanged man's right to a last word.'

Then the door was flung open.

'Is that you, doña Eduviges?' I called. 'What's going on? Were you afraid?'

'My name isn't Eduviges. I am Damiana. I heard you were here and I've come to see you. I want you to come sleep at my house. You'll be able to rest there.'

'Damiana Cisneros? Aren't you one of the women who lived at the Media Luna?'

'I do live there. That's why it took me so long to get here.'

'My mother told me about a woman named Damiana who looked after me when I was born. Was that you?'

'Yes. I'm the one. I've known you since you first opened your eyes.'

'I'll be glad to come. I can't get any rest here because of the yelling. Didn't you hear it? How they were murdering someone? Didn't you hear it just now?'

'It may be some echo trapped in here. A long time ago they hanged Toribio Aldrete in this room. Then they locked the door and left him to turn to leather. So he would never find rest. I don't know how you got in, when there isn't any key to open this door.'

'It was doña Eduviges who opened it. She told me it was the only room she had available.'

'Eduviges Dyada?'

'Yes, she was the one.'

'Poor Eduviges. That must mean she's still wandering like a lost soul.'

'I, Fulgor Sedano, fifty-four years of age, bachelor, administrator by profession and skilled in filing and prosecuting lawsuits, by the power invested in me and by my own authority, do claim and allege the following ...'

That was what he had written when he filed the complaint against deeds committed by Toribio Aldrete. And he had ended: 'The charge is falsifying boundaries.'

'There's no one can call you less than a man, don Fulgor. I know you can hold your own. And not because of the power behind you, but on your own account.'

He remembered. That was the first thing Aldrete had told him after they began drinking together, reputedly to celebrate the complaint:

'We'll wipe our asses with this paper, you and I, don Fulgor, because that's all it's good for. You know that. In other words, as far as you're concerned, you've done your part and cleared the air. Because you had me worried, which anyone might be. But now I know what it's all about, it makes me laugh. Falsify boundaries? Me? If he's that stupid, your *patrón* should be red in the face.'

He remembered. They had been at Eduviges' place. He had even asked her:

'Say, 'Viges. Can you let me have the corner room?'

'Whatever rooms you want, don Fulgor. If you want, take them all. Are your men going to spend the night?'

'No, I just need one. Don't worry about us, go on to bed. Just leave us the key.'

'Well, like I told you, don Fulgor,' Toribio Aldrete had said. 'There's no one can doubt your manhood, but I'm fuckin' well fed up with that shit-ass son of your *patrón*.'

He remembered. It was the last thing he heard with all his wits about him. Later, he had acted like a coward, yelling, 'Power behind me, you say? 's'at right?'

He used the butt of his whip to knock at Pedro Páramo's door. He thought of the first time he had done that, two weeks earlier. He waited, as he had that first time. And again as he had then, he examined the black bow hanging above the door. But he did not comment again: 'Well, how about that! They've hung one over the other. The first one's faded now, but the new one shines like silk, even though you can see it's just something they've dyed.'

That first time he had waited so long that he'd begun to think maybe no one was home. He was just leaving when Pedro Páramo finally appeared.

'Come in, my friend.'

It was the second time they had met. The first time only he had been aware of the meeting because it was right after little Pedro was born. And this time. You might almost say it was the first time. And here he was being treated like an equal. How about that! Fulgor followed with long strides, slapping his whip against his leg. He'll soon learn that I'm the man who knows what's what. He'll learn. And know why I've come.

'Sit down, Fulgor. We can speak at our ease here.'

They were in the horse corral. Pedro Páramo made himself comfortable on a feed trough, and waited.

'Don't you want to sit down?'

'I prefer to stand, Pedro.'

'As you like. But don't forget the don.'

Who did the boy think he was to speak to him like that? Not even his father, don Lucas Páramo, had dared do that. So the very first thing, this kid, who had never stepped foot on the Media Luna or done a lick of work, was talking to him as if he were a hired hand. How about *that*!

'So, what shape is this operation in?'

Sedano felt this was his opportunity 'Now it's my turn,' he thought.

'Not so good. There's nothing left. We've sold off the last head of cattle.'

He began taking out papers to show Pedro Páramo how much he owed. And he was just ready to say, 'We owe such and such,' when he heard the boy ask:

'Who do we owe it *to*? I'm not interested in how much, just who to.'

Fulgor ran down the list of names. And ended: 'There's nowhere to get the money to pay. That's the crux of the problem.'

'Why not?'

'Because your family ate it all up. They borrowed and borrowed without ever returning any of it. One day you have to pay the piper. I always used to say, "One of these days they're going to have everything there is." Well, that's what happened. Now, I know someone who might be interested in buying the land. They'll pay a good price. It will cover your outstanding debts, with a little left over. Though not very much.'

'That "someone" wouldn't be you?'

'What makes you think it's me?'

'I'm suspicious of my own shadow. Tomorrow morning we'll begin to set our affairs in order. We'll begin with the Preciado women. You say it's them we owe the most?'

'Yes. And them we've paid the least. Your father always left the Preciados to the last. I understand that one of the girls, Matilde, went to live in the city. I don't know whether it was Guadalajara or Colima. And that Lola, that is, doña Dolores, has been left in charge of everything. You know, of don Enmedio's ranch. She's the one we have to pay.'

'Then tomorrow I want you to go and ask for Lola's hand.'

'What makes you think she'd have me? I'm an old man.'

'You'll ask her for me. After all, she's not without her charms. Tell her I'm very much in love with her. Ask her if she likes the idea. And on the way, ask Father Rentería to make the arrangements. How much money can you get together?'

'Not a centavo, don Pedro.'

'Well, promise him something. Tell him the minute I have any money, I'll pay him. I'm pretty sure he won't stand in the way. Do it tomorrow. Early.'

'And what about Aldrete?'

'What does Aldrete have to do with anything? You told me about the Preciado women, and the Fregosos and the Guzmáns. So what's this about Aldrete?'

'It's the matter of the boundaries. He's been putting up fences, and now he wants us to put up the last part in order to establish the property lines.'

'Leave that for later. You're not to worry about fences. There're not going to be any fences. The land's not to be divided up. Think about that, Fulgor, but don't tell anyone just yet. For now, first thing, set it up with Lola. Sure you won't sit down?'

'I will, don Pedro. God's truth, I'm beginning to like working with you.'

'You string Lola a line, and tell her I love her. That's important. It's true, Sedano, I do love her. Because of her eyes, you know? You do that first thing in the morning. And I'll relieve you of some of your administrative duties. You can leave the Media Luna to me.'

I wonder where in hell the boy learned those tricks, Fulgor Sedano thought on his second trip to the Media Luna. I never expected anything from him. 'He's worthless,' my old *patrón* don Lucas used to say. 'A born weakling.' And I couldn't argue. 'When I die, Fulgor, you look for another job.' 'I will, don Lucas.' 'I tell you, Fulgor, I tried sending him to the seminary, hoping that at least he would have enough to eat and could look after his mother when I'm no longer here. But he didn't even stick with that.' 'You deserve better, don Lucas.' 'Don't count on him for anything, not even to care for me when I'm old. He's turned out bad, Fulgor, and that's that.' 'That's a real shame, don Lucas.'

And now this. If the Media Luna hadn't meant so much to him, he'd never have called on Miguel. He'd have left without contacting him. But he loved that land: the barren hills that had been worked year in and year out and still accepted the plough, giving more every year ... Beloved Media Luna ... And each new addition, like Enmedio's land: 'Come to me, sweetheart.' He could see it, as easy as if it were already done. And what does a woman matter, after all. 'Damn right!' he said, slapping the whip against his leg as he walked through the main door of the hacienda.

It had been easy enough to gull Dolores. Her eyes shone and her face showed her discomposure.

'Forgive me for blushing, don Fulgor. I can't believe don Pedro ever noticed me.'

'He can't sleep for thinking about you.'

'But he has so many to choose from. There are so many pretty girls in Comala. What will they say when they find out?'

'He thinks of no one but you, Dolores. Nobody but you.'

'You give me the shivers, don Fulgor. I never dreamed ...'

'It's because he's a man of so few words. Don Lucas Páramo, may he rest in peace, actually told him you weren't good enough for him. So out of obedience he kept his silence. But now his father's gone, there's nothing to stand in the way. It was his first decision – although I've been slow to carry it out because of all the things I had to do. We'll set the wedding for day after tomorrow. How does that suit you?'

'Isn't that awfully soon? I don't have anything ready. I'll need time to get my trousseau together. I'll want to write my sister. No, I'll send her a letter by messenger. But no matter what, I won't be ready before the eighth of April. Today is the first. Yes, the earliest would be the eighth. Ask him to wait just a few short days longer.'

'He wishes it were this minute. If it's just a matter of your wedding dress, we'll provide that. Don Pedro's dear dead mother would want you to have hers. It's a family custom.'

'But there's another reason I want those extra days. It's a woman's matter, you know. Oh! I'm so embarrassed to say this, don Fulgor. My face must be a hundred colours. But it's my time of the month. Oh, I'm so ashamed.'

'What does that have to do with it? Marriage isn't a question of your time or not your time. It's a matter of loving each other. When you have that, nothing else matters.'

'But you don't understand what I'm saying, don Fulgor.'

'I understand. The wedding will be day after tomorrow.'

And he left her with arms outstretched, begging for one week, just one week.

I mustn't forget to tell don Pedro – God, that Pedro's a sharp boy! – I musn't forget to tell him, remember to tell the judge to put the property in joint ownership. Don't forget, now, Fulgor, to tell him first thing tomorrow.

Meanwhile, Dolores was running to the kitchen with a water jug to set water to boil. 'I'll have to try to bring it on sooner. This very night. But whatever I do, it will still last three days. There's no way around it. But oh, I'm so happy. So happy! Thank you, God, for giving me don Pedro.' And then she added. 'Even if later he does get tired of me.'

'I've asked her, and she's for it. The priest wants sixty pesos to overlook the matter of the banns. I told him he'd get it in due time. He says he needs it to fix the altar, and that his dining room table is on its last legs. I promised that we'd send him a new table. He says you never come to mass. I promised him you would. And since your grandmother died, he says, no one over here has tithed. I told him not to worry. He'll go along.'

'You didn't ask for a little advance from Dolores?'

'No, *patrón*. I didn't dare. That's the truth. She was so happy I didn't want to dim her enthusiasm.'

'What a baby you are.'

A baby he says? Me, with all my fifty-five years? Look at him, just beginning to live, and me only a few steps from the grave. 'I didn't want to spoil her happiness.'

'In spite of everything, you're still a kid.'

'Anything you say, *patrón*.'

'Next week, I want you to go over to see Aldrete. Tell him to check his fences. He's on Media Luna land.'

'He did a good job measuring the boundary lines. I can vouch for that.'

'Well, tell him he made a mistake. That he didn't figure right. If necessary, tear down the fences.'

'And the law?'

'What law, Fulgor? From now on, we're the law. Do you have any roughnecks working on the Media Luna?'

'Well, there's one or two.'

'Send them over to do business with Aldrete. You draw up a complaint accusing him of squatting on our land, or whatever occurs to you. And remind him that Lucas Páramo is dead. And that from now on he'll be dealing with me.'

There were only a few clouds in the still-blue sky. Higher up, air was stirring but down below it was still and hot.

Again he knocked with the butt of the whip, if only to assert his presence, since he knew by now that no one would open until Pedro Páramo fancied. Seeing the black bows above the door, he thought: Those ribbons look pretty; one for each.

At that moment the door opened, and he stepped inside.

'Come in, Fulgor. Did you take care of Toribio Aldrete?'

'That job's done, *patrón*.'

'We still have the matter of the Fregosos. We'll let that ride. Right now I'm all wrapped up in my honeymoon.'

'This town is filled with echoes. It's like they were trapped behind the walls, or beneath the cobblestones. When you walk you feel like someone's behind you, stepping in your footsteps. You hear rustlings. And people laughing. Laughter that sounds used up. And voices worn away by the years. Sounds like that. But I think the day will come when those sounds fade away.'

That was what Damiana Cisneros was telling me as we walked through the town.

'There was a time when night after night I could hear the sounds of a fiesta. I could hear the noise clear out at the Media Luna. I would walk into town to see what the uproar was about, and this is what I would see: just what we're seeing now. Nothing. No one. The streets as empty as they are now.

'Then I didn't hear anything anymore. You know, you can get worn out celebrating. That's why I wasn't surprised when it ended.

'Yes,' Damiana Cisneros repeated. 'This town is filled with echoes. I'm not afraid anymore. I hear the dogs howling, and I let them howl. And on windy days I see the wind blowing leaves from the trees, when anyone can see that there aren't any trees here. There must have been once. Otherwise, where do the leaves come from?

'And the worst of all is when you hear people talking and the voices seem to be coming through a crack, and yet so clear you can recognize who's speaking. In fact, just now as I was coming here I happened upon a wake. I stopped to recite the Lord's Prayer. And while I was praying, one woman stepped away from the others and came toward me and said, "Damiana! Pray for me, Damiana!"

'Her rebozo fell away from her face and I recognized my sister Sixtina.

'"What are you doing here?" I asked her.

'Then she ran back and hid among the other women.

'In case you didn't know, my sister Sixtina died when I was twelve years old. She was the oldest. There were sixteen of us, so you can figure how long she's been dead. And look at her now, still wandering through this world. So don't be afraid if you hear newer echoes, Juan Preciado.'

'Was it my mother who told you I was coming?' I asked.

'No. And by the way, whatever happened to your mother?'

'She died,' I replied.

'Died? What of?'

'I don't really know. Sadness, maybe. She sighed a lot.'

'That's bad. Every sigh is like a drop of your life being swallowed up. Well, so she's dead.'

'Yes. I thought maybe you knew.'

'Why would I know? I haven't heard a thing from her in years.'

'Then how did you know about me?'

Damiana did not answer.

'Are you alive, Damiana? Tell me, Damiana!'

Suddenly I was alone in those empty streets. Through the windows of roofless houses you could see the tough stems of tall weeds. And meagre thatch revealing crumbling adobe.

'Damiana!' I called. 'Damiana Cisneros!'

The echo replied: '... ana ... neros! ... ana ... neros!'

I heard dogs barking, as if I had roused them. I saw a man crossing the street.

'Hey, you!' I called.

'Hey, you!' came back my own voice.

And as if they were just around the next corner, I heard two women talking:

'Well, look who's coming toward us. Isn't that Filoteo Aréchiga?'

'The very one. Pretend you don't see him.'

'Even better, let's leave. And if he walks after us, it means he wants something of one of us. Which one of us do you think he's following?'

'It must be you.'

'Well, I figure it's you he wants.'

'Oh, we don't have to run anymore. He stopped back on the corner.'

'Then it wasn't either of us. You see?'

'But what if it had been? What then?'

'Don't get ideas.'

'It's a good thing he didn't. Everyone says that he's the one who gets the girls for don Pedro. Which just missed being us.'

'Is that right? Well, I don't want to have anything to do with that old man.'

'We better go.'

'Yes, let's. Let's go home.'

Night. Long after midnight. And the voices:

'I'm telling you that if we have a good corn crop this year I'll be able to pay you. But if we lose it, well, you'll just have to wait.'

'I'm not pushing you. You know I've been patient with you. But it's not your land. You've been working land that's not yours. So where are you going to get the money to pay me?'

'And who says the land isn't mine?'

'I heard you sold it to Pedro Páramo.'

'I haven't been anywhere near him. The land's still mine.'

'That's what you say. But everyone is saying it's his.'

'Just let them say that to me.'

'Look, Galileo, just between the two of us, in confidence, I like you a lot. After all, you're my sister's husband. And I never heard anyone say you don't treat her well. But don't try to tell me you didn't sell the land.'

'I do tell you, I haven't sold it to anyone.'

'Well, it belongs to Pedro Páramo. I know that's how he means it to be. Didn't don Fulgor come see you?'

'No.'

'Then you can be sure he'll be here tomorrow. And if not tomorrow, some day soon.'

'Then one of us will die, but he's not going to get his way on this.'

'Rest in peace, Amen, dear brother-in-law. Just in case.'

'I'll be around, you'll see. Don't worry about me. My mother tanned my hide enough to make me good and tough.'

''Til tomorrow, then. Tell Felicitas that I won't be to dinner tonight. I wouldn't want to have to say later, "I was with him the night before he died."'

'We'll save something for you in case you change your mind at the last minute.'

Receding footsteps sounded to the jingle of spurs.

'Tomorrow morning at dawn you're coming with me, Chona. I have the team hitched up.'

'And what if my father has a fit and dies? As old as he is … I'd never forgive myself if something happened to him because of me. I'm the only one he has to see that he takes care of himself. There's no one else. Why are you in such a hurry to steal me from him? Wait just a little longer. It won't be long till he dies.'

'That's what you told me last year. You even taunted me for not being willing to take a chance, and from what you said then, you were fed up with everything. I've harnessed the mules and they're ready. Are you coming with me?'

'Let me think about it.'

'Chona! You don't know how much I want you. I can't stand it any longer, Chona. One way or another, you're coming with me.'

'I need to think about it. Try to understand. We have to wait until he dies. It won't be long now. Then I'll go with you and we won't have to run away.'

'You told me that, too, a year ago.'

'And so?'

'Chona, I had to hire the mules. They're ready. They're just waiting for you. Let him get along on his own. You're pretty. You're young. Some old woman will come look after him. There's more than enough kind souls to go around.'

'I can't.'

'Yes you can.'

'I can't. It hurts me, you know that. But he is my father.'

'Then there's nothing more to say. I'll go see Juliana, she's crazy about me.'

'Fine. I won't tell you not to.'

'Then you don't want to see me tomorrow?'

'No. I don't ever want to see you again.'

Sounds. Voices. Murmurs. Distant singing:

My sweetheart gave me a lace-bordered
handkerchief to dry my tears ...

High voices. As if it were women singing.

I watched the carts creaking by. The slowly moving oxen. The crunching of stones beneath the wheels. The men, seeming to doze.

... Every morning early the town trembles from the passing carts. They come from everywhere, loaded with nitre, ears of corn, and fodder. The wheels creak and groan until the windows rattle and wake the people inside. That's also the hour when the ovens are opened and you can smell the new-baked bread. Suddenly it will thunder. And rain. Maybe spring's on its way. You'll get used to the 'suddenlys' there, my son.

Empty carts, churning the silence of the streets. Fading into the dark road of night. And shadows. The echo of shadows.

I thought of leaving. Up the hill I could sense the track I had followed when I came, like an open wound through the blackness of the mountains.

Then someone touched my shoulder.

'What are you doing here?'

'I came to look for ...' I was going to say the name, but stopped. 'I came to look for my father.'

'Why don't you come in?'

I went in. Half the roof had fallen in on the house. The tiles lay on the ground. The roof on the ground. And in the other half were a man and a woman.

'Are you dead?' I asked them.

The woman smiled. The man's gaze was serious.

'He's drunk,' the man said.

'He's just scared,' said the woman.

There was an oil stove. A bamboo cot, and a crude chair where the woman's clothes were laid. Because she was naked, just as God had sent her into the world. And the man, too.

'We heard someone moaning and butting his head against our door. And there you were. What happened to you?'

'So many things have happened that all I want to do is sleep.'

'That's what we were doing.'

'Let's all sleep, then.'

My memories began to fade with the light of dawn.

From time to time I heard the sound of words, and marked a difference. Because until then, I realized, the words I had heard had been silent. There had been no sound, I had sensed them. But silently, the way you hear words in your dreams.

'Who could he be?' the woman was asking.

'Who knows?' the man replied.

'I wonder what brought him here?'

'Who knows?'

'I think I heard him say something about his father.'

'I heard him say that, too.'

'You don't think he's lost? Remember when those people happened by who said they were lost? They were looking for a place called Los Confines, and you told them you didn't know where it was.'

'Yes, I remember. But let me sleep. It's not dawn yet.'

'But it will be before long. And I'm talking to you because I want you to wake up. You told me to remind you before dawn. That's why I'm doing it. Get up!'

'Why do you want me to get up?'

'I don't know why. You told me last night to wake you. You didn't tell me why.'

'If that's your only reason, let me sleep. Didn't you hear what the man said when he came? To let him sleep. That was all he had to say.'

It seemed as if the voices were moving away. Fading. Being choked off. No one was saying anything now. It was a dream.

But after a while, it began again:

'He moved. I'll bet he's about to wake up. And if he sees us here he'll ask questions.'

'What questions can he ask?'

'Well. He'll have to say something, won't he?'

'Leave him alone. He must be very tired.'

'You think so?'

'That's enough, woman.'

'Look, he's moving. See how he's tossing? Like something inside him was jerking him around. I know because that's happened to me.'

'What's happened to you?'

'That.'

'I don't know what you're talking about.'

'I wouldn't mention it except that when I see him tossing in his sleep like that I remember what happened to me the first time you did it to me. How it hurt, and how bad I felt about doing it.'

'What do you mean, "it"?'

'How I felt right after you did it to me, and how, whether you like it or not, I knew it wasn't done right.'

'Are you going to start that again? Why don't you go to sleep, and let me sleep, too.'

'You asked me to remind you. That's what I'm doing. Dear God, I'm doing what you asked me to. Come on! It's almost time for you to get up.'

'Leave me alone, woman.'

The man seemed to sleep. The woman kept on scolding, but in a quiet voice:

'It must be after dawn by now, because I can see light. I can see that man from here, and if I can see him it's only because there's enough light to see. The sun will be up before long. I don't need to tell you that. What do you bet he's done something wrong. And we took him in. It doesn't matter that it was only for tonight; we hid him. And in the long run that will mean trouble for us ... Look how restless he is, as if he can't get comfortable. I'll bet he has a heavy load on his soul.'

It was growing lighter. Day was routing the shadows. Erasing them. The room where I lay was warm with the heat of sleeping bodies. I sensed the dawn light through my eyelids. I felt the light. I heard:

'He's thrashing around like he's damned. He has all the

earmarks of an evil man. Get up, Donis! Look at him. Look how he's writhing there on the ground, twisting and turning. He's drooling. He must have killed a lot of people. And you didn't even see it.'

'Poor devil. Go to sleep ... and let us sleep!'

'And how can I sleep if I'm not sleepy?'

'Get up, then, and go somewhere you won't be pestering me!'

'I will. I'll go light the fire. And as I go I'll tell what's-his-name to come sleep here by you, here in my place.'

'You tell him that.'

'I can't. I'd be afraid to.'

'Then go about your work and leave us alone.'

'I'm going to.'

'What are you waiting for?'

'I'm on my way.'

I heard the woman get out of bed. Her bare feet thudded on the ground and she stepped over my head. I opened and closed my eyes.

When I opened them again, the sun was high in the sky. Beside me sat a clay jug of coffee. I tried to drink it. I took a few swallows.

'It's all we have. I'm sorry it's so little. We're so short of everything, so short ...'

It was a woman's voice.

'Don't worry on my account,' I told her. 'Don't worry about me. I'm used to it. How do I get out of here?'

'Where are you going?'

'Anywhere.'

'There's dozens of roads. One goes to Contla, and there's another one comes from there. One leads straight to the mountains. I don't know where the one goes you can see from here,' and she pointed past the hole in the roof, the place where the roof had fallen in. 'That other one down there goes past the Media Luna. And there's still another that runs the length of the place; that's the longest.'

'Then that may be the way I came.'

'Where are you heading?'

'Toward Sayula.'

'Imagine. I thought Sayula was that way. I always wanted to go there. They say there's lots of people there.'

'About like other places.'

'Think of that. And us all alone here. Dying to know even a little of life.'

'Where did your husband go?'

'He isn't my husband. He's my brother, though he doesn't want anyone to know. Where did he go? I guess to look for a stray calf that's been wandering around here. At least that's what he told me.'

'How long have you two been here?'

'Forever. We were born here.'

'Then you must have known Dolores Preciado.'

'Maybe *he* did, Donis. I know so little about people. I never go out. I've been right here for what seems forever. Well, maybe not that long. Just since he made me his woman. Ever since then, I've been closed up here, because I'm afraid to be seen. He doesn't want to believe it, but isn't it true I would give anyone a scare?' She walked to stand in the sunlight. 'Look at my face!'

It was an ordinary face.

'What is it you want me to see?'

'Don't you see my sin? Don't you see those purplish spots? Like impetigo? I'm covered with them. And that's only on the outside; inside, I'm a sea of mud.'

'But who's going to see you if there's no one here? I've been through the whole town and not seen anyone.'

'You think you haven't, but there are still a few people around. Haven't you seen Filomeno? Or Dorotea or Melquiades or old Prudencio? And aren't Sóstenes and all of them still alive? What happens is that they stay close to home. I don't know what they do by day, but I know they spend their nights locked up indoors. Nights around here are filled with ghosts. You should see all the spirits walking through the streets. As soon as it's dark they begin to come out. No one likes to see them. There's so many of them and so few of us that we don't even make the effort to pray for them anymore, to help them out of their purgatory. We don't have enough prayers to go around. Maybe a few words of the Lord's Prayer for each one. But that's not going to do them any good. Then there are our sins on top of theirs. None of us still living is in God's grace. We can't lift up our eyes, because they're filled with shame. And shame doesn't help. At least that's what the Bishop said. He came through here some time ago giving confirmation, and I went to him and confessed everything:

'"I can't pardon you," he said.

'"I'm filled with shame."

'"That isn't the answer."

'"Marry us!"

'"Live apart!"

'I tried to tell him that life had joined us together, herded us like animals, forced us on each other. We were so alone here; we were the only two left. And somehow the village had to have people again. I told him now maybe there would be someone for him to confirm when he came back.

'"Go your separate ways. There's no other way."

'"But how will we live?"

'"Like anyone lives."

'And he rode off on his mule, his face hard, without looking back, as if he was leaving an image of damnation behind him. He's never come back. And that's why this place is swarming with spirits: hordes of restless souls who died without forgiveness, and, people would never have won forgiveness in any case – even less if they had to depend on us. He's coming. You hear?'

'Yes, I hear.'

'It's him.'

The door opened.

'Did you find the calf?' she asked.

'It took it in its head not to come, but I followed its tracks and I'll soon find where it is. Tonight I'll catch it.'

'You're going to leave me alone at night?'

'I may have to.'

'But I can't stand it. I need you here with me. That's the only time I feel comfortable. That time of night.'

'But tonight I'm going after the calf.'

'I just learned,' I interrupted, 'that you two are brother and sister.'

'You just learned that? I've known it a lot longer than you. So don't be sticking your nose into it. We don't like people talking about us.'

'I only mentioned it to show I understand. That's all.'

'Understand what?'

The woman went to stand beside him, leaning against his shoulder, and repeated in turn:

'You understand what?'

'Nothing,' I said. 'I understand less by the minute.' And added: 'All I want is to go back where I came from. I should use what little light's left of the day.'

'You'd better wait,' he told me. 'Wait till morning. It'll be dark soon, and all the roads are grown over. You might get lost. I'll start you off in the right direction tomorrow.'

'All right.'

Through the hole in the roof I watched the thrushes, those birds that flock at dusk before the darkness seals their way. Then, a few clouds already scattered by the wind that comes to carry off the day.

Later the evening star came out; then, still later, the moon.

The man and woman were not around. They had gone out through the patio and by the time they returned it was already dark. So they had no way of knowing what had happened while they were gone.

And this was what happened:

A woman came into the room from the street. She was ancient, and so thin she looked as if her hide had shrunk to her bones. She looked around the room with big round eyes. She may even have seen me. Perhaps she thought I was sleeping. She went straight to the bed and pulled a leather trunk from beneath it. She searched through it. Then she clutched some sheets beneath her arm and tiptoed out as if not to wake me.

I lay rigid, holding my breath, trying to look anywhere but at her. Finally I worked up the courage to twist my head and look in her direction, toward the place where the evening star had converged on the moon.

'Drink this,' I heard.

I did not dare turn my head.

'Drink it! It will do you good. It's orange-blossom tea. I know you're scared because you're trembling. This will ease your fright.'

I recognized the hands, and as I raised my eyes I recognized the face. The man, who was standing behind her, asked:

'Do you feel sick?'

'I don't know. I see things and people where you may not see anything. A woman was just here. You must have seen her leave.'

'Come on,' he said to his wife. 'Leave him alone. He talks like a mystic.'

'We should let him have the bed. Look how he's trembling. He must have a fever.'

'Don't pay him any mind. People like him work themselves into a state to get attention. I knew one over at the Media Luna who called himself a divine. What he never "divined" was that he was going to die as soon as the *patrón* "divined" what a bungler he was. This one's just like him. They spend their lives going from town to town "to see what the Good Lord has to offer," but he'll not find anyone here to give him so much as a bite to eat. You see how he stopped trembling? He hears what we're saying.'

It was as if time had turned backward. Once again I saw the star nesting close to the moon. Scattering clouds. Flocks of thrushes. And suddenly, bright afternoon light.

Walls were reflecting the afternoon sun. My footsteps sounded on the cobblestones. The burro driver was saying, 'Look up doña Eduviges, if she's still alive!'

Then a dark room. A woman snoring by my side. I noticed that her breathing was uneven, as if she were dreaming, or as if she were awake and merely imitating the sounds of sleep. The cot was a platform of poles covered with gunnysacks that smelled of piss, as if they'd never been aired in the sun. The pillow was a saddle pad wrapped around a log or a roll of wool so hard and sweaty it felt as solid as a rock.

I could feel a woman's naked legs against my knee, and her breath upon my face. I sat up in the bed, supporting myself on the adobe-hard pillow.

'You're not asleep?' she asked.

'I'm not sleepy. I slept all day long. Where's your brother?'

'He went off somewhere. You heard him say where he had to go. He may not come back tonight.'

'So he went anyway? In spite of what you wanted?'

'Yes. And he may never come back. That's how they all do. "I have to go down there; I have to go on out that way." Until they've gone so far that it's easier not to come back. He's been trying and trying to leave, and I think this is the time. Maybe, though he didn't say so, he left me here for you to take care of. He saw his chance. The business of the stray was just an excuse. You'll see. He's not coming back.'

I wanted to say, 'I feel dizzy. I'm going out to get a little air.' Instead, I said:

'Don't worry. He'll be back.'

When I got out of bed, she said:

'I left something for you on the coals in the kitchen. It's not very much, but it will at least keep you from starving.'

I found a piece of dried beef, and a few warm tortillas.

'That's all I could get,' I heard her saying from the other room. 'I traded my sister two clean sheets I've had since my mother died. I kept them under the bed. She must have come to get them. I didn't want to tell you in front of Donis, but she was the woman you saw ... the one who gave you such a scare.'

A black sky, filled with stars. And beside the moon the largest star of all.

'Don't you hear me?' I asked in a low voice.

And her voice replied: 'Where are you?'

'I'm here, in your village. With your people. Don't you see me?'

'No, son. I don't see you.'

Her voice seemed all-encompassing. It faded into distant space.

'I don't see you.'

I went back to the room where the woman was sleeping and told her:

'I'll stay over here in my own corner. After all, the bed's as hard as the floor. If anything happens, let me know.'

'Donis won't be back,' she said. 'I saw it in his eyes. He was waiting for someone to come so he could get away. Now you'll be the one to look after me. Won't you? Don't you want to take care of me? Come sleep here by my side.'

'I'm fine where I am.'

'You'd be better off up here in the bed. The ticks will eat you alive down there.'

I got up and crawled in bed with her.

The heat woke me just before midnight. And the sweat. The woman's body was made of earth, layered in crusts of earth; it was crumbling, melting into a pool of mud. I felt myself swimming in the sweat streaming from her body, and I couldn't get enough air to breathe. I got out of bed. She was sleeping. From her mouth bubbled a sound very like a death rattle.

I went outside for air, but I could not escape the heat that followed wherever I went.

There was no air; only the dead, still night fired by the dog days of August.

Not a breath. I had to suck in the same air I exhaled, cupping it in my hands before it escaped. I felt it, in and out, less each time ... until it was so thin it slipped through my fingers forever.

I mean, forever.

I have a memory of having seen something like foamy clouds swirling above my head, and then being washed by the foam and sinking into the thick clouds. That was the last thing I saw.

'Are you trying to make me believe you drowned, Juan Preciado? I found you in the town plaza, far from Donis's house, and he was there, too, telling me you were playing dead. Between us we dragged you into the shadow of the arches, already stiff as a board, and all drawn up like a person who'd died of fright. If there hadn't been any air to breathe that night you're talking about, we wouldn't have had the strength to carry you, even less bury you. And, as you see, bury you we did.'

'You're right, Doroteo. You say your name's Doroteo?'

'It doesn't matter. It's really Dorotea. But it doesn't matter.'

'It's true, Dorotea. The murmuring killed me.'

There you'll find the place I love most in the world. The place where I grew thin from dreaming. My village, rising from the plain. Shaded with trees and leaves like a piggy bank filled with memories. You'll see why a person would want to live there forever. Dawn, morning, midday, night: always the same, except for the changes in the air. The air changes the colour of things there. And life whirs by as quiet as a murmur ... the pure murmuring of life ...

'Yes, Dorotea. The murmuring killed me. I was trying to hold back my fear. But it kept building until I couldn't contain it any longer. And when I was face to face with the murmuring, the dam burst.

'I went to the plaza. You're right about that. I was drawn there by the sound of people; I thought there really were people. I wasn't in my right mind by then. I remember I got there by feeling my way along the walls as if I were walking with my hands. And the walls seemed to distil the voices, they seemed to be filtering through the cracks and crumbling mortar. I heard them. Human voices: not clear, but secretive voices that seemed to be whispering something to me as I passed, like a buzzing in my ears. I moved away from the walls and continued down the middle of the street. But I still heard them; they seemed to be keeping pace with me – ahead of me, or just behind me. Like I told you, I wasn't hot anymore. Just the opposite, I was cold. From the time I left the house of that woman who let me use her bed, the one – I told you – I'd seen dissolving in the liquid of her sweat, from that time on I'd felt cold. And the farther I walked, the colder I got, until my skin was all goose bumps. I wanted to turn back; I thought that if I went back I might find the warmth I'd left behind; but I realized after I walked a bit farther that the cold was coming from me, from my own blood. Then I realized I was afraid. I heard all the noise in the plaza, and I thought I'd find people there to help me get over my fear. That's how you came to find me in the plaza. So Donis came back? The woman was sure she'd never see him again.'

'It was morning by the time we found you. I don't know where he came from. I didn't ask him.'

'Well, anyway, I reached the plaza. I leaned against a pillar of the arcade. I saw that no one was there, even though I could still hear the murmuring of voices, like a crowd on market day. A steady sound with no words to it, like the sound of the wind through the branches of a tree at night, when you can't see the tree or the branches but you hear the whispering. Like that. I couldn't take another step. I began to sense that whispering drawing nearer, circling around me, a constant buzzing like a swarm of bees, until finally I could hear the almost soundless words 'Pray for us.' I could hear that's what they were saying to me. At that moment, my soul turned to ice. That's why you found me dead.'

'You'd have done better to stay home. Why did you come here?'

'I told you that at the very beginning. I came to find Pedro Páramo, who they say was my father. Hope brought me here.'

'Hope? You pay dear for that. My illusions made me live longer than I should have. And that was the price I paid to find my son, who in a manner of speaking was just one more illusion. Because I never had a son. Now that I'm dead I've had time to think and understand. God never gave me so much as a nest to shelter my baby in. Only an endless life-time of dragging myself from pillar to post, sad eyes casting sidelong glances, always looking past people, suspicious that this one or that one had hidden my baby from me. And it was all the fault of one bad dream. I had two: one of them I call the "good dream," and the other the "bad dream." The first was the one that made me dream I had a son to begin with. And as long as I lived, I always believed it was true. I could feel him in my arms, my sweet baby, with his little mouth and eyes and hands. For a long, long time I could feel his eyelids, and the beating of his heart, on my fingertips. Why wouldn't I think it was true? I carried him with me everywhere I went, wrapped in my rebozo, and then one day I lost him. In heaven they told me they'd made a mistake. That they'd given me a mother's heart but the womb of a whore. That was the other dream I had. I went up to heaven and peeked in to see whether I could recognize my son's face among the angels. Nothing. The faces were all the same, all made from the same mould. Then I asked. One of those saints came over to me and, without a word, sank his hand into my stomach, like he would have poked into a ball of wax. When he pulled out his hand he showed me something that looked like a nutshell. "This proves what I'm demonstrating to you."

'You know how strange they talk up there, but you can understand what they're saying. I wanted to tell them that it was just my stomach, all dried up from hunger and nothing to eat, but another one of those saints took me by the shoulders and pushed me to the door. "Go rest a while more on earth, my daughter, and try to be good so that your time in purgatory will be shortened."

'That was my "bad dream," and the one where I learned I never had a son. I learned it very late, after my body had already shrivelled up and my backbone jutted up higher than the top of my head and I couldn't walk anymore. And to top it off, everyone was leaving the village; all the people set out for somewhere else and took their charity with them. I sat down to wait for death. After we found you, my bones determined to find their rest. "No one will notice me," I thought. "I won't be a bother to anyone." You see, I didn't even steal space from the earth. They buried me in the grave with you, and I fit right in the hollow of your arms. Here in this little space where I am now. The only thing is that probably I should have my arms around *you*. You hear? It's raining up there. Don't you hear the drumming of the rain?'

'I hear something like someone walking above us.'

'You don't have to be afraid. No one can scare you now. Try to think nice thoughts, because we're going to be a long time here in the ground.'

At dawn a heavy rain was falling over the earth. It thudded dully as it struck the soft loose dust of the furrows. A mockingbird swooped low across the field and wailed, imitating a child's plaint; a little farther it sang something that sounded like a sob of weariness and in the distance where the horizon had begun to clear, it hiccupped and then laughed, only to wail once more.

Fulgor Sedano breathed in the scent of fresh earth and looked out to see how the rain was penetrating the furrows.

His little eyes were happy. He took three deep gulps, relishing the savour, and grinned till his teeth showed.

'Ahhh!' he said. 'We're about to have another good year.' And then added: 'Come on down, rain. Come on down. Fall until you can't fall anymore! And then move on. Remember that we worked the ground just to pleasure you.'

And he laughed aloud.

Returning from its survey of the fields, the mockingbird flew past him and wailed a heartrending wail.

The rain intensified until in the distance where it had begun to grow light the clouds closed in, and it seemed that the darkness that had been retreating was returning.

The huge gate of the Media Luna squealed as it swung open, wet from the moist wind. First two, then another two, then two more rode out, until two hundred men on horseback had scattered across the rain-soaked fields.

'We'll have to drive the Enmedio herd up past where Estagua used to be, and the Estagua cattle up to the Vilmayo hills,' Fulgor Sedano ordered as the men rode by. 'And hurry, the rain's really coming down!'

He said it so often that the last to leave heard only, 'From here to there, and from there, farther on up.'

Every man of them touched the brim of his hat to show that he had understood.

Almost immediately after the last man had left, Miguel Páramo galloped in at full tilt and without reining in his horse dismounted almost in Fulgor's face, leaving his mount to find its own way to the stall.

'Where've you been at this hour, boy?'

'Been doing a little milking.'

'Milking who?'

'You can't guess?'

'Must have been that Dorotea. *La Cuarraca*. She's the only one around here likes babies.'

'You're a fool, Fulgor. But it's not your fault.'

And without bothering to remove his spurs, Miguel went off to find someone to feed him breakfast.

In the kitchen Damiana Cisneros asked him the same question:

'Now where've you been, Miguel?'

'Oh, just around. Calling on the mothers of the region.'

'I didn't mean to rile you, Miguel. How do you want your eggs.'

'Could I have them with a special side dish?'

'I'm being serious, Miguel.'

'I know, Damiana. Don't worry. Listen. Do you know a woman named Dorotea? The one they call *La Cuarraca*?'

'I do. And if you want to see her, you'll find her right outside. She gets up early every morning to come by here for her breakfast. She's the one who rolls up a bundle in her rebozo and sings to it, and calls it her baby. It must be that something terrible happened to her a long while back, but since she never talks, no one knows what it was. She lives on handouts.'

'That damned Fulgor! I'm going to give him a lick that'll make his eyes whirl.'

He sat and thought for a while, wondering how the woman might be of use to him. Then without further hesitation he went to the back kitchen door and called Dorotea:

'Come here a minute, I've got a proposition to make you,' he said.

Who knows what deal he offered her; the fact is that when he came inside he was rubbing his hands.

'Bring on those eggs!' he yelled to Damiana. And added: 'From now on, I want you to give that woman the same food you give me, and if it makes extra work, it's no problem of mine.'

In the meantime, Fulgor Sedano had gone to check the amount of grain left in the bins. Since harvest was a long way off, he was worried about the shrinking supply. In fact, the crops were barely in the ground. 'I have to see if we can get by.' Then he added: 'That boy! A ringer for his father, all right, but he's starting off too early. At this rate, I don't think he'll last. I forgot to tell him that yesterday someone came by and said he'd killed a man. If he keeps up like this ...'

He sighed and tried to imagine where the ranch hands would be by now. But he was distracted by Miguel Páramo's young chestnut stallion, rubbing its muzzle against the corral fence. 'He never even unsaddled his horse,' he thought. 'And he doesn't intend to. At least don Pedro is more reliable, and he has his quiet moments. He sure indulges Miguel, though. Yesterday when I told him what his son had done, he said, "Just think of it as something I did, Fulgor. The boy couldn't have done a thing like that; he doesn't have the guts yet to kill a man. That takes balls this big." And he held his hands apart

70

as if he was measuring a squash. Anything he does, you can lay it on me.'

'Miguel's going to give you a lot of headaches, don Pedro. He likes to wrangle.'

'Give him his head. He's just a boy. How old is he now? Going on seventeen, Fulgor?'

'About that. I can remember when they brought him here; it seems like yesterday. But he's wild, and he lives so fast that sometimes it appears to me he's racing with time. He'll be the one to lose that game. You'll see.'

'He's still a baby, Fulgor.'

'Whatever you say, don Pedro; but that woman who came here yesterday, weeping and accusing your son of killing her husband, was not to be consoled. I know how to judge grief, don Pedro, and that woman was carrying a heavy load. I offered her a hundred and fifty bushels of maize to overlook the matter, but she wouldn't take it. Then I promised we'd make things right somehow. She still wasn't satisfied.'

'What was it all about?'

'I don't know the people involved.'

'There's nothing to worry about, Fulgor. Those people don't really count.'

Fulgor went to the storage bins, where he could feel the warmth of the maize. He took a handful and examined it to see whether it had been infested with weevils. He measured the height in the bins. 'It'll do,' he said. 'As soon as we have grass we won't have to feed grain anymore. So there's more than enough.'

As he walked back he gazed at the overcast sky. 'We'll have rain for a good while.' And he forgot about everything else.

'The weather must be changing up there. My mother used to tell me how as soon as it began to rain everything was filled with light and with the green smell of growing things. She told me how the waves of clouds drifted in, how they emptied themselves upon the earth and transformed it, changing all the colours. My mother lived her childhood and her best years in this town, but couldn't even come here to die. And so she sent me in her place. It's strange, Dorotea, how I never saw the sky. At least it should have been the sky she knew.'

'I don't know, Juan Preciado. After so many years of never lifting up my head, I forgot about the sky. And even if I had looked up, what good would it have done? The sky is so high and my eyes so clouded that I was happy just knowing where the ground was. Besides, I lost all interest after padre Rentería told me I would never know glory. Or even see it from a distance ... It was because of my sins, but he didn't have to tell me that. Life is hard enough as it is. The only thing that keeps you going is the hope that when you die you'll be lifted off this mortal coil; but when they close one door to you and the only one left open is the door to Hell, you're better off not being born ... For me, Juan Preciado, heaven is right here.'

'And your soul? Where do you think it's gone?'

'It's probably wandering like so many others, looking for living people to pray for it. Maybe it hates me for the way I treated it, but I don't worry about that anymore. And now I don't have to listen to its whining about remorse. Because of it, the little I ate turned bitter in my mouth; it haunted my nights with black thoughts of the damned. When I sat down to die, my soul prayed for me to get up and drag on with my life, as if it still expected some miracle to cleanse me of my sins. I didn't even try. "This is the end of the road," I told it. "I don't have the strength to go on." And I opened my mouth to let it escape. And it went. I knew when I felt the little thread of blood that bound it to my heart drip into my hands.'

They pounded at his door, but he didn't answer. He heard them knock at door after door, waking everyone around. Fulgor – he knew him by his footsteps – paused a moment as he hurried toward the main door, as if he meant to knock again. Then kept running.

Voices. Slow, scraping footsteps, like people carrying a heavy load.

Unidentifiable sounds.

His father's death came to his mind. It had been an early dawn like this, although that morning the door had been open and he had seen the grey of a dismal, ashen sky seeping through. And a woman had been leaning against the door frame, trying to hold back her sobs. A mother he had forgotten, forgotten many times over, was telling him: 'They've killed your father!' In a broken quavering voice held together only by the thread of her sobs.

He never liked to relive that memory because it brought

others with it, as if a bulging sack of grain had burst and he was trying to keep the kernels from spilling out. The death of his father dragged other deaths with it, and in each of them was always the image of that shattered face: one eye mangled, the other staring vengefully. And another memory, and another, until that death was erased from memory and there was no longer anyone to remember it.

'Lay him down here. No, not like that. Put his head that way. You! What are you waiting for?'

All this in a low voice.

'Where's don Pedro?'

'He's sleeping. Don't wake him. Don't make any noise.'

But there he stood, towering, watching them struggle with a large bundle wrapped in old gunnysacks and bound with hemp like a shroud.

'Who is it?' he asked.

Fulgor Sedano stepped forward and said:

'It's Miguel, don Pedro.'

'What did they do to him?' he shouted.

He was expecting to hear 'They killed him.' And he felt the stirrings of rage forming hard lumps of rancour; instead he heard Fulgor Sedano's soft voice saying:

'No one did anything to him. He met his death alone.'

Oil lamps lighted the night.

'His horse killed him,' one man volunteered.

They laid him out on his bed; they turned back the mattress and exposed the bare boards, and arranged the body now free of the bonds they had used to carry it home. They crossed his hands over his chest and covered his face with a black cloth. 'He looks bigger than he was,' Fulgor thought to himself.

Pedro Páramo stood there, his face empty of expression, as if he were far away. Somewhere beyond his consciousness, his thoughts were racing, unformed, disconnected. At last he said:

'I'm beginning to pay. The sooner I begin, the sooner I'll be through.'

He felt no sorrow.

When he spoke to the people gathered in the patio, to thank them for their presence, making his voice heard above the wailing of the women, he was not short either of breath or of words. Afterward, the only sound was that of the pawing of Miguel Páramo's chestnut stallion.

'Tomorrow,' he ordered Fulgor Sedano, 'get someone to put that animal down and take him out of his misery.'

'Right, don Pedro. I understand. The poor beast must be suffering.'

'That's my feeling, too, Fulgor. And as you go, tell those women not to make such a racket; they're making too much fuss over my loss. If it was their own, they wouldn't be so eager to mourn.'

Years later Father Rentería would remember the night his hard bed had kept him awake and driven him outside. It was the night Miguel Páramo died.

He had wandered through the lonely streets of Comala, his footsteps spooking the dogs sniffing through the garbage heaps. He walked as far as the river, where he stood gazing at how stars falling from the heavens were reflected in the quiet eddies. For several hours he struggled with his thoughts, casting them into the black waters of the river.

It had all begun, he thought, when Pedro Páramo, from the low thing he was, made something of himself. He flourished like a weed. And the worst of it is that I made it all possible. 'I have sinned, padre. Yesterday I slept with Pedro Páramo.' 'I have sinned, padre. I bore Pedro Páramo's child.' 'I gave my daughter to Pedro Páramo, padre.' I kept waiting for him to come and confess something, but he never did. And then he extended the reach of his evil through that son of his. The one he recognized – only God knows why. What I do know is that I placed that instrument in his hands.

He remembered vividly the day he had brought the child to Pedro Páramo, only hours old.

He had said to him:

'Don Pedro, the mother died as she gave birth to this baby. She said that he's yours. Here he is.'

Pedro Páramo never even blinked; he merely said:

'Why don't you keep him, Father? Make a priest out of him.'

'With the blood he carries in his veins, I don't want to take that responsibility.'

'Do you really think he has bad blood?'

'I really do, don Pedro.'

'I'll prove you wrong. Leave him here with me. I can find someone to take care of him.'

'That's just what I had in mind. At least he'll eat if he's with you.'

Tiny as he was, the infant was writhing like a viper.

'Damiana! Here's something for you to take care of. It's my son.'

Later he had uncorked a bottle:

'This one's for the deceased, and for you.'

'And for the child?'

'For him, too. Why not?'

He filled another glass and both of them drank to the child's future.

That was how it had been.

Carts began rumbling by toward the Media Luna. Father Rentería crouched low, hiding in the reeds along the river's edge. 'What are you hiding from?' he asked himself.

'Adios, padre,' he heard someone say.

He rose up and answered:

'Adios! May God bless you.'

The lights in the village went out one by one. The river was glowing with luminous colour.

'Padre, has the Angelus rung yet?' asked one of the drivers.

'It must be much later than that,' he replied. And he set off in the opposite direction, vowing not to be stopped.

'Where are you off to so early, padre?'

'Where's the death, padre?'

'Did someone in Contla die, padre?'

He felt like answering, 'I did. I'm the one who's dead.' But he limited himself to a smile.

As he left the last houses behind, he walked faster.

It was late morning when he returned.

'Where have you been, Uncle,' his niece Ana asked. 'A lot of women have been here looking for you. They wanted to confess; tomorrow's the first Friday.'

'Tell them to come back this evening.'

He sat for a quiet moment on a bench in the hall, heavy with fatigue.

'How cool the air is, Ana.'

'It's very warm, Uncle.'

'I don't feel it.'

The last thing he wanted to think about was that he had been in Contla, where he had made a general confession to a fellow priest who despite his pleas had refused him absolution.

'That man whose name you do not want to mention has destroyed your church, and you have allowed him to do it. What can I expect of you now, Father? How have you used God's might? I want to think that you're a good man and that you're held in high esteem because of that. But it's not enough to be good. Sin is not good. And to put an end to sin, you must be hard and merciless. I want to think that your parishioners are still believers, but it is not you who sustains their faith. They believe out of superstition and fear. I feel very close to you in your penury, and in the long hours you spend every day carrying out your duties. I personally know how difficult our task is in these miserable villages to which we have been banished; but that in itself gives me the right to tell you that we cannot serve only the few who give us a pittance in exchange for our souls. And with your soul in their hands, what chance do you have to be better than those who are better than you? No, Father, my hands are not sufficiently clean to grant you absolution. You will have to go elsewhere to find that.'

'What do you mean? That I must look somewhere else if I want to confess?'

'Yes, you must. You cannot continue to consecrate others when you yourself are in sin.'

'But what if they remove me from my ministry?'

'Maybe you deserve it. They will be the ones to judge.'

'Couldn't you …? Provisionally, I mean … I must administer the last rites … give communion. So many are dying in my village, Father.'

'Oh, my friend, let God judge the dead.'

'Then you won't absolve me?'

And the priest in Contla had told him no.

Later the two of them had strolled through the azalea-shaded cloister of the parish patio. They sat beneath an arbour where grapes were ripening.

'They're bitter, Father,' the priest anticipated Father Rentería's question. 'We live in a land in which everything grows, thanks to God's providence; but everything that grows is bitter. That is our curse.'

'You're right, father. I've tried to grow grapes over in Comala. They don't bear. Only guavas and oranges: bitter oranges and bitter guavas. I've forgotten the taste of sweet fruit. Do you remember the China guavas we had in the seminary? The peaches? The tangerines that shed their skin at a touch? I brought seeds here. A few, just a small pouch.

Afterward, I felt it would have been better to leave them where they were, since I only brought them here to die.'

'And yet, Father, they say that the earth of Comala is good. What a shame the land is all in the hands of one man. Pedro Páramo is still the owner, isn't he?'

'That is God's will.'

'I can't believe that the will of God has anything to do with it. You don't believe that, do you, Father?'

'At times I have doubted; but they believe it in Comala.'

'And are you among the "they"?'

'I am just a man prepared to humble himself, now while he has the impulse to do so.'

Later, when they said their good-byes, Father Rentería had taken the priest's hands and kissed them. Now that he was home, and returned to reality, he did not want to think about the morning in Contla.

He rose from the bench and walked to the door.

'Where are you going, Uncle?'

His niece Ana, always present, always by his side, as if she sought his shadow to protect her from life.

'I'm going out to walk for a while, Ana. To blow off steam.'

'Do you feel sick?'

'Not sick, Ana. Bad. I feel that's what I am. A bad man.'

He walked to the Media Luna and offered his condolences to Pedro Páramo. Again he listened to his excuses for the charges against his son. He let Pedro Páramo talk. None of it mattered, after all. On the other hand, he did decline his invitation to eat.

'I can't do that, don Pedro. I have to be at the church early because a long line of women are already waiting at the confessional. Another time.'

He walked home, then toward evening went directly to the church, just as he was, bathed in dust and misery. He sat down to hear confessions.

The first woman in line was old Dorotea, who was always waiting for the church doors to open.

He smelled the odour of alcohol.

'What? Now you're drinking? How long have you been doing this?'

'I went to Miguelito's wake, padre. And I overdid it a little. They gave me so much to drink that I ended up acting like a clown.'

'That's all you've ever done, Dorotea.'

'But now I've come with my sins, padre. Sins to spare.'

On many occasions he had told her, 'Don't bother to confess, Dorotea; you'd be wasting my time. You couldn't commit a sin anymore, even if you tried. Leave that to others.'

'I have now, padre. It's the truth.'

'Tell me.'

'Since it can't do him any harm now, I can tell you that I'm the one who used to get the girls for the deceased. For Miguelito Páramo.'

Father Rentería, stalling for time to think, seemed to emerge from his fog as he asked, almost from habit:

'For how long?'

'Ever since he was a boy. From that time he had the measles.'

'Repeat to me what you just said, Dorotea.'

'Well, that I was the one who rounded up Miguelito's girls.'

'You took them to him?'

'Sometimes I did. Other times I just made the arrangements. And with some, all I did was head him in the right direction. You know, the hour when they would be alone, and when he could catch them unawares.'

'Were there many?'

He hadn't meant to ask, but the question came out by force of habit.

'I've lost count. Lots and lots.'

'What do you think I should do with you, Dorotea? You be the judge. Can you pardon what you've done?'

'I can't, padre. But you can. That's why I'm here.'

'How many times have you come to ask me to send you to Heaven when you die? You hoped to find your son there, didn't you, Dorotea? Well, you won't go to Heaven now. May God forgive you.'

'Thank you, padre.'

'Yes. And I forgive you in His name. You may go.'

'Aren't you going to give me any penance?'

'You don't need it, Dorotea.'

'Thank you, padre.'

'Go with God.'

He rapped on the window of the confessional to summon another of the women. And while he listened to 'I have sinned,' his head slumped forward as if he could no longer hold it up. Then came the dizziness, the confusion, the slipping away as if in syrupy water, the whirling lights; the brilliance of the dying day was splintering into shards. And there was the taste of blood on his tongue. The 'I have sinned' grew louder, was repeated again and again: 'for now and forever more,' 'for now and forever more,' 'for now ...'

'Quiet, woman,' he said. 'When did you last confess?'

'Two days ago, padre.'

Yet she was back again. It was as if he were surrounded by misfortune. What are you doing here, he asked himself. Rest. Go rest. You are very tired.

He left the confessional and went straight to the sacristy. Without a glance for the people waiting, he said:

'Any of you who feel you are without sin may take Holy Communion tomorrow.'

Behind him, as he left, he heard the murmuring.

I am lying in the same bed where my mother died so long ago; on the same mattress, beneath the same black wool coverlet she wrapped us in to sleep. I slept beside her, her little girl, in the special place she made for me in her arms.

I think I can still feel the calm rhythm of her breathing; the palpitations and sighs that soothed my sleep ... I think I feel the pain of her death ... But that isn't true.

Here I lie, flat on my back, hoping to forget my loneliness by remembering those times. Because I am not here just for a while. And I am not in my mother's bed but in a black box like the ones for burying the dead. Because I am dead.

I sense where I am, but I can think ...

I think about the limes ripening. About the February wind

that used to snap the fern stalks before they dried up from neglect. The ripe limes that filled the overgrown patio with their fragrance.

The wind blew down from the mountains on February mornings. And the clouds gathered there waiting for the warm weather that would force them down into the valley. Meanwhile the sky was blue, and the light played on little whirlwinds sweeping across the earth, swirling the dust and lashing the branches of the orange trees.

The sparrows were twittering; they pecked at the wind-blown leaves, and twittered. They left their feathers among the thorny branches, and chased the butterflies, and twittered. It was that season.

February, when the mornings are filled with wind and sparrows and blue light. I remember. That is when my mother died.

I should have wailed. I should have wrung my hands until they were bleeding. That is how you would have wanted it. But in fact, wasn't that a joyful morning? The breeze was blowing in through the open door, tearing loose the ivy tendrils. Hair was beginning to grow on the mound between my legs, and my hands trembled hotly when I touched my breasts. Sparrows were playing. Wheat was swaying on the hillside. I was sad that she would never again see the wind playing in the jasmines; that her eyes were closed to the bright sunlight. But why should I weep?

Do you remember, Justina? You arranged chairs in a row in the corridor where the people who came to visit could wait their turn. They stood empty. My mother lay alone amid the candles; her face pale, her white teeth barely visible between purple lips frozen by the livid cold of death. Her eyelashes lay still; her heart was still. You and I prayed interminable prayers she could not hear, that you and I could not hear above the roar of the wind in the night. You ironed her black dress, starched her collar and the cuffs of her sleeves so her hands would look young crossed upon her dead breast – her exhausted, loving breast that had once fed me, that had cradled me and throbbed as she crooned me to sleep.

No one came to visit her. Better that way. Death is not to be parcelled out as if it were a blessing. No one goes looking for sorrow.

Someone banged the door knocker. You went to the door.

'You go,' I said. 'I see people through a haze. Tell them to go away. Have they come for money for the Gregorian masses? She didn't leave any money. Tell them that, Justina. Will she have to stay in purgatory if they don't say those masses? Who are they to mete out justice, Justina? You think I'm crazy? That's fine.'

And your chairs stood empty until we went to bury her, accompanied by the men we had hired, sweating under a stranger's weight, alien to our grief. They shovelled damp sand into the grave; they lowered the coffin, slowly, with the patience of their office, in the breeze that cooled them after their labours. Their eyes cold, indifferent. They said: 'It'll be so much.' And you paid them, the way you might buy something at the market, untying the corner of the tear-soaked handkerchief you'd wrung out again and again, the one that now contained the money for the burial ...

And when they had gone away, you knelt on the spot above her face and you kissed the ground, and you would have dug down toward her if I hadn't said: 'Let's go, Justina. She isn't here now. There's nothing here but a dead body.'

'Was that you talking, Dorotea?'

'Who, me? I was asleep for a while. Are you still afraid?'

'I heard someone talking. A woman's voice. I thought it was you.'

'A woman's voice? You thought it was me? It must be that woman who talks to herself. The one in the large tomb. Doña Susanita. She's buried close to us. The damp must have got to her, and she's moving around in her sleep.'

'Who is she?'

'Pedro Páramo's last wife. Some say she was crazy. Some say not. The truth is that she talked to herself even when she was alive.'

'She must have died a long time ago.'

'Oh, yes! A long time ago. What did you hear her say?'

'Something about her mother.'

'But she didn't have a mother ...'

'Well, it was her mother she was talking about.'

'Hmmm. At least, her mother wasn't with her when she came. Wait a minute. I remember now the mother was born here, and when she was getting along in years, they vanished. Yes, that's it. Her mother died of consumption. She was a strange woman who was always sick and never visited with anyone.'

'That's what she was saying. That no one had come to visit her mother when she died.'

'What did she mean? No wonder no one wanted to step inside her door, they were afraid of catching her disease. I wonder if the Indian woman remembers?'

'She was talking about that.'

'When you hear her again, let me know. I'd like to know what she's saying.'

'You hear? I think she's about to say something. I hear a kind of murmuring.'

'No, that isn't her. That's farther away and in the other direction. And that's a man's voice. What happens with these corpses that have been dead a long time is that when the damp reaches them they begin to stir. They wake up.'

'The heavens are bountiful. God was with me that night. If not, who knows what might have happened. Because it was already night when I came to ...'

'You hear it better now?'

'Yes.'

'... I was covered with blood. And when I tried to get up my hands slipped in the puddles of blood in the rocks. It was my blood. Buckets of blood. But I wasn't dead. I knew that. I knew that don Pedro hadn't meant to kill me. Just give me a scare. He wanted to find out whether I'd been in Vilmayo that day two years before. On San Cristobal's day. At the wedding. What wedding? Which San Cristobal's? There I was slipping around in my own blood, and I asked him just that: "What wedding, don Pedro? No! No, don Pedro. I wasn't there. I may have been near there, but only by chance ... He never meant to kill me. He left me lame – you can see that – and, sorry to say, without the use of my arm. But he didn't kill me. They say that ever since then I've had one wild eye. From the scare. I tell you, though, it made me more of a man. The heavens are bountiful. And don't you ever doubt it.'"

'Who was that?'

'How should I know? Any one of dozens. Pedro Páramo slaughtered so many folks after his father was murdered that he killed nearly everybody who attended that wedding. Don Lucas Páramo was supposed to give the bride away. And it was really by accident that he died, because it was the bridegroom someone had a grudge against. And since they never found out who fired the bullet that struck him down, Pedro Páramo wiped out the lot. It happened over there on Vilmayo ridge, where there used to be some houses you can't find any trace of now ... Listen ... Now that sounds like her. Your ears are younger. You listen. And then tell me what she says.'

'I can't understand a thing. I don't think she's talking; just moaning.'

'What's she moaning about?'

'Well, who knows.'

'It must be about something. No one moans just to be moaning. Try harder.'

'She's moaning. Just moaning. Maybe Pedro Páramo made her suffer.'

'Don't you believe it. He loved her. I'm here to tell you that he never loved a woman like he loved that one. By the time they brought her to him, she was already suffering – maybe crazy. He loved her so much that after she died he spent the rest of his days slumped in a chair, staring down the road where they'd carried her to holy ground. He lost interest in everything. He let his lands lie fallow, and gave orders for the tools that worked it to be destroyed. Some say it was because he was worn out; others said it was despair. The one sure thing is that he threw everyone off his land and sat himself down in his chair to stare down that road.

'From that day on the fields lay untended. Abandoned. It was a sad thing to see what happened to the land, how plagues took over as soon as it lay idle. For miles around, people fell on hard times. Men packed up and left in search of a better living. I remember days when the only sound in Comala was good-byes; it seemed like a celebration every time we sent someone on his way. They went, you know, with every intention of coming back. They asked us to keep an eye on their belongings and their families. Later, some sent for their family but not their things. And then they seemed to forget about the village, and about us – and even about their belongings. I stayed because I didn't have anywhere to go. Some stayed waiting for Pedro Páramo to die, because he'd promised to leave them his land and his goods and they were living on that hope. But the years went by and he lived on, propped up like a scarecrow gazing out across the lands of the Media Luna.

'And not long before he died we had that Cristeros war, and

the troops drained off the few men he had left. That was when I really began to starve, and things were never the same again.

'And all of it was don Pedro's doing, because of the turmoil of his soul. Just because his wife, that Susanita, had died. So you tell me whether he loved her.'

It was Fulgor Sedano who told him:

'*Patrón*. You know who's back in town?'

'Who?'

'Bartolomé San Juan.'

'How come?'

'That's what I asked myself. Wonder why he's come back?'

'Haven't you looked into it?'

'No. I wanted to tell you first. He didn't inquire about a house. He went straight to your old place. He got off his horse and moved in his suitcases, just as if you'd already rented it to him. He didn't seem to have any doubts.'

'And what are you doing about it, Fulgor? Why haven't you found out what's going on? Isn't that what you're paid to do?'

'I was a little thrown off by what I just told you. But tomorrow I'll find out, if you think we should.'

'Never mind about tomorrow. I'll look into the San Juans. Both of them came?'

'Yes. Him and his wife. But how did you know?'

'Wasn't it his daughter?'

'Well, the way he treats her, she seems more like his wife.'

'Go home and go to bed, Fulgor.'

'With your leave.'

I waited thirty years for you to return, Susana. I wanted to have it all. Not just part of it, but everything there was to have, to the point that there would be nothing left for us to want, no desire but your wishes. How many times did I ask your father to come back here to live, telling him I needed him. I even tried deceit.

I offered to make him my administrator, anything, as long as I could see you again. And what did he answer? 'No response,' the messenger always said. 'Señor don Bartolomé tears up your letters as soon as I hand them to him.' But through that boy I learned that you had married, and before long I learned you were a widow and had gone back to keep your father company.

Then silence.

The messenger came and went, and each time he reported: 'I can't find them, don Pedro. People say they've left Mascota. Some say they went in one direction, and some say another.'

I told him: 'Don't worry about the expense. Find them. They haven't been swallowed up by the earth.'

And then one day he came and told me:

'I've been all through the mountains searching for the place where don Bartolomé San Juan might be hiding and at last I found him, a long way from here, holed up in a little hollow in the hills, living in a log hut on the site of the abandoned La Andromeda mines.'

Strange winds were blowing then. There were reports of armed rebellion. We heard rumours. Those were the winds that blew your father back here. Not for his own sake, he wrote in his letter, but your safety. He wanted to bring you back to civilization.

I felt that the heavens were parting. I wanted to run to meet you. To envelop you with happiness. To weep with joy. And weep I did, Susana, when I learned that at last you would return.

'Some villages have the smell of misfortune. You know them after one whiff of their stagnant air, stale and thin like everything old. This is one of those villages, Susana.

'Back there, where we just came from, at least you could enjoy watching things being born: clouds and birds and moss. You remember? Here there's nothing but that sour, yellowish odour that seems to seep up from the ground. This town is cursed, suffocated in misfortune.

'He wanted us to come back. He's given us his house. He's given us everything we need. But we don't have to be grateful to him. This is no blessing for us, because our salvation is not to be found here. I feel it.

'Do you know what Pedro Páramo wants? I never imagined that he was giving us all this for nothing. I was ready to give him the benefit of my toil, since we had to repay him somehow. I gave him all the details about La Andromeda, and convinced him that the mine had promise if we worked it methodically. You know what he said? "I'm not interested in your mine, Bartolomé San Juan. The only thing of yours I want is your daughter. She's your crowning achievement."

'He loves you, Susana. He says you used to play together

when you were children. That he knows you. That you used to swim together in the river when you were young. I didn't know that. If I'd known I would have beat you senseless.'

'I'm sure you would.'

'Did I hear what you said? "I'm sure you would"?'

'You heard me.'

'So you're prepared to go to bed with him?'

'Yes, Bartolomé.'

'Don't you know that he's married, and that he's had more women than you can count?'

'Yes, Bartolomé.'

'And don't call me Bartolomé! I'm your father!'

Bartolomé San Juan, a dead miner. Susana San Juan, daughter of a miner killed in the Andromeda mines. He saw it clearly. 'I must go there to die,' he thought. Then he said:

'I've told him that although you're a widow, you are still living with your husband – or at least you act as if you are. I've tried to discourage him, but his gaze grows hard when I talk to him, and as soon as I mention your name, he closes his eyes. He is, I haven't a doubt of it, unmitigated evil. That's who Pedro Páramo is.'

'And who am I?'

'You are my daughter. Mine. The daughter of Bartolomé San Juan.'

Ideas began to form in Susana San Juan's mind, slowly at first; they retreated and then raced so fast she could only say:

'It isn't true. It isn't true.'

'This world presses in on us from every side; it scatters

fistfuls of our dust across the land and takes bits and pieces of us as if to water the earth with our blood. What did we do? Why have our souls rotted away? Your mother always said that at the very least we could count on God's mercy. Yet you deny it, Susana. Why do you deny me as your father? Are you mad?'

'Didn't you know?'

'Are you mad?'

'Of course I am, Bartolomé. Didn't you know?'

'You know of course, Fulgor, that she is the most beautiful woman on the face of the earth. I had come to believe I had lost her forever. I don't want to lose her again. You understand me, Fulgor? You tell her father to go explore his mines. And there ... I imagine it wouldn't be too hard for an old man to disappear in a territory where no one ever ventures. Don't you agree?'

'Maybe so.'

'We need it to be so. She must be left without family. We're called on to look after those in need. You agree with that, don't you?'

'I don't see any difficulty with that.'

'Then get about it, Fulgor. Get on with it.'

'And what if she finds out?'

'Who's going to tell her? Let's see, tell me. Just between the two of us, who's going to tell her?'

'No one, I guess.'

'Forget the "I guess." Forget that as of now, and everything'll work out fine. Remember how much needs to be done at the Andromeda. Send the old man there to keep at it. To come and go as he pleases. But don't let him get the idea of taking his daughter. We'll look after her here. His work is there in the mines and his house is here anytime he wants it. Tell him that, Fulgor.'

'I'd like to say once more that I like the way you do things, *patrón*. You seem to be getting your spirit back.'

Rain is falling on the fields of the valley of Comala. A fine rain, rare in these lands that know only downpours. It is Sunday. The Indians have come down from Apango with their rosaries of chamomile, their rosemary, their bunches of thyme. They have come without ocote pine, because the wood is wet, and without oak mulch, because it, too, is wet from the long rain. They spread their herbs on the ground beneath the arches of the arcade. And wait.

The rain falls steadily, stippling the puddles.

Rivers of water course among the furrows where the young maize is sprouting. The men have not come to the market today; they are busy breaching the rows so the water will find new channels and not carry off the young crop. They move in groups, navigating the flooded fields beneath the rain, breaking up soft clumps of soil with their spades, firming the shoots with their hands, trying to protect them so they will grow strong.

The Indians wait. They feel this is an ill-fated day. That may be why they are trembling beneath their soaking wet *gabanes*, their straw capes – not from cold, but fear. They stare at the fine rain and at the sky hoarding its clouds.

No one comes. The village seems uninhabited. A woman asks for a length of darning cotton, and a packet of sugar, and, if it is to be had, a sieve for straining cornmeal gruel. As the morning passes, the *gabanes* grow heavy with moisture. The Indians talk among themselves, they tell jokes, and laugh. The chamomile leaves glisten with a misting of rain. They think, 'If only we'd brought a little puque, it wouldn't matter; but the hearts of the magueys are swimming in a sea of water. Well, what can you do?'

Beneath her umbrella Justina Díaz makes her way down the straight road leading from the Media Luna, avoiding the streams of water gushing onto the sidewalks. As she passed the main entry to the church, she made the sign of the cross. She walked beneath the arches into the plaza. All the Indians turned to watch her. She felt their eyes upon her, as if she were under intense scrutiny. She stopped at the first display of herbs, bought ten centavos worth of rosemary, and then retraced her steps, followed by countless pairs of Indian eyes.

'Everything costs so much this time of year,' she thought as she walked back toward the Media Luna. 'This pitiful little bunch of rosemary for ten centavos. It's barely enough to give off a scent.'

Toward dusk the Indians rolled up their wares. They walked into the rain with their heavy packs on their backs. They stopped by the church to pray to the Virgin, leaving a bunch of thyme as an offering. Then they set off toward Apango, on their way home. 'Another day,' they said. And they walked down the road telling jokes, and laughing.

Justina Díaz went into Susana San Juan's bedroom and set the rosemary on a small shelf. The closed curtains blocked out the light, so that she saw only shadows in the darkness; she merely guessed at what she was seeing. She supposed that Susana San Juan was asleep; she wished that she did nothing but sleep, and as she was sleeping now, Justina was content. But then she heard a sigh that seemed to come from a far corner of the darkened room.

'Justina!' someone called.

She looked around. She couldn't see anyone but she felt a hand on her shoulder and a breath against her ear. A secretive voice said, 'Go away, Justina. Bundle up your things, and leave. We don't need you anymore.'

'She needs me,' she replied, standing straighter. 'She's sick, and she needs me.'

'Not anymore, Justina. I will stay here and take care of her.'

'Is that you, don Bartolomé?' But she did not wait for the answer. She screamed a scream that reached the ears of men and women returning from the fields, a cry that caused them to say 'That sounded like someone screaming but it can't be human.'

The rain deadens sounds. It can be heard when all other sound is stilled, flinging its icy drops, spinning the thread of life.

'What's the matter, Justina? Why did you scream?' Susana San Juan asked.

'I didn't scream, Susana. You must have been dreaming.'

'I've told you, I never dream. You have no consideration. I scarcely slept a wink. You didn't put the cat out last night, and it kept me awake.'

'It slept with me, between my legs. It got wet, and I felt sorry for it and let it stay in my bed; but it didn't make any noise.'

'No, it didn't make any noise. But it spent the night like a circus cat, leaping from my feet to my head, and meowing softy as if it were hungry.'

'I fed it well, and it never left my bed all night. You've been dreaming lies again, Susana.'

'I tell you, it kept startling me all night with its leaping about. Your cat may be very affectionate, but I don't want it around when I'm sleeping.'

'You're seeing things, Susana. That's what it is. When Pedro Páramo comes, I'm going to tell him that I can't put up with you any longer. I'll tell him I'm leaving. There are plenty of nice people who will give me work. Not all of them are crazy like you, or enjoy humiliating a person the way you do. Tomorrow morning I'm leaving; I'll take my cat and leave you in peace.'

'You won't leave, you perverse and wicked Justina. You're not going anywhere, because you will never find anyone who loves you the way I do.'

'No, I won't leave, Susana. I won't leave. You know I will take care of you. Even though you make me swear I won't, I will always take care of you.'

She had cared for Susana from the day she was born. She had held her in her arms. She had taught her to walk. To take those first steps that seemed eternal. She had watched her lips and eyes grow sweet as sugar candy. 'Mint candy is blue. Yellow and blue. Green and blue. Stirred with spearmint and wintergreen.' She nibbled at her chubby legs. She entertained her by offering her a breast to nurse that had no milk, that was only a toy. 'Play with this,' she told Susana. 'Play with your own little toy.' She could have hugged her to pieces.

Outside, rain was falling on the banana leaves and water in the puddles sounded as if it were boiling.

The sheets were cold and damp. The drainpipes gurgled and foamed, weary of labouring day and night, day and night. Water kept pouring down, streaming in diluvial burbling.

It was midnight; outside, the sound of the rain blotted out all other sounds.

Susana San Juan woke early. She sat up slowly, then got out of bed. Again she felt the weight in her feet, a heaviness rising up her body, trying to reach her head:

'Is that you, Bartolomé?'

She thought she heard the door squeak, as if someone were entering or leaving. And then only the rain, intermittent, cold, rolling down the banana leaves, boiling in its own ferment.

She slept again and did not wake until light was falling on red bricks beaded with moisture in the grey dawn of a new day. She called:

'Justina!'

Justina, throwing a shawl around her shoulders, appeared immediately, as if she had been right outside the door.

'What is it, Susana?'

'The cat. The cat's in here again.'

'My poor Susana.'

She laid her head on Susana's breast and hugged her until Susana lifted her head and asked 'Why are you crying? I'll tell Pedro Páramo how good you are to me. I won't tell him anything about how your cat frightens me. Don't cry, Justina.'

'Your father's dead, Susana. He died night before last. They came today to say there's nothing we can do; they've already buried him. It was too far to bring his body back here. You're all alone now, Susana.'

'Then it was Father,' Susana smiled. 'So he came to tell me good-bye,' she said. And smiled.

Many years earlier, when she was just a little girl, he had said one day:

'Climb down, Susana, and tell me what you see.'

She was dangling from a rope that cut into her waist and rubbed her hands raw, but she didn't want to let go. That rope was the single thread connecting her to the outside world.

'I don't see anything, papá.'

'Look hard, Susana. See if you don't see something.'

And he shone the lamp on her.

'I don't see anything, papá.'

'I'll lower you a little farther. Let me know when you're on the bottom.'

She had entered through a small opening in some boards. She had walked over rotted, decaying, splintered planks covered with clayey soil:

'Go a little lower, Susana, and you'll find what I told you.'

She bumped lower and lower, swaying in the darkness, with her feet swinging in empty space.

'Lower, Susana. A little lower. Tell me if you see anything.'

And when she felt the ground beneath her feet she stood there dumb with fear. The lamplight circled above her and then focused on a spot beside her. The yell from above made her shiver:

'Hand me that, Susana!'

She picked up the skull in both hands, but when the light struck it fully, she dropped it.

'It's a dead man's skull,' she said.

'You should find something else there beside it. Hand me whatever's there.'

The skeleton broke into individual bones: the jawbone fell away as if it were sugar. She handed it up to him, piece after piece, down to the toes, which she handed him joint by joint. The skull had been first, the round ball that had disintegrated in her hands.

'Keep looking, Susana. For money. Round gold coins. Look everywhere, Susana.'

And then she did not remember anything, until days later she came to in the ice: in the ice of her father's glare.

That was why she was laughing now.

'I knew it was you, Bartolomé.'

And poor Justina, weeping on Susana's bosom, sat up to see what she was laughing about and why her laughter had turned to wild guffaws.

Outside, it was still raining. The Indians had gone. It was Monday and the valley of Comala was drowning in rain.

The winds continued to blow, day after day. The winds that had brought the rain. The rain was over but the wind remained. There in the fields, tender leaves, dry now, lay flat against the furrows, escaping the wind. By day the wind was bearable; it worried the ivy and raided the roof tiles; but by night it moaned, it moaned without ceasing. Canopies of clouds swept silently across the sky, so low they seemed to scrape the earth.

Susana San Juan heard the wind lashing against the closed window. She was lying with her arms crossed behind her head, thinking, listening to the night noises: how the night was buffeted by bursts of restless wind. Then the abrupt cessation.

Someone has opened the door. A rush of air blows out the lamp. She sees only darkness, and conscious thought is suspended. She hears faint rustlings. The next moment she hears the erratic beating of her heart. Through closed eyelids she senses the flame of light.

She does not open her eyes. Her hair spills across her face. The light fires drops of sweat on her upper lip. She asks:

'Is that you, Father?'

'Yes, I am your father, my child.'

She peers through half-closed eyelids. Her hair seems to be cloaking a shadowy figure on the ceiling, its head looming above her face. Through the haze of her eyelashes a blurred figure takes form. A diffuse light burns in the place of its heart, a tiny heart pulsing like a flickering flame. 'Your heart is dying of pain,' Susana thinks. 'I know that you've come to tell me Florencio is dead, but I already know that. Don't be sad about anything else; don't worry about me. I keep my grief hidden in a safe place. Don't let your heart go out!'

She got out of bed and dragged herself toward Father Rentería.

'Let me console you,' he said, protecting the flame of the candle with his cupped hand, 'console you with my own inconsolable sorrow.'

Father Rentería watched as she approached him and encircled the lighted flame with her hands, and then she lowered her face to the burning wick until the smell of burning flesh forced him to jerk the candle away and blow out the flame.

Again in darkness, Susana ran to hide beneath the sheets.

Father Rentería said:

'I have come to comfort you, daughter.'

'Then you may go, Father,' she replied. 'Don't come back. I don't need you.'

And she listened to the retreating footsteps that had always left a sensation of cold and fear.

'Why do you come see me, when you are dead?'

Father Rentería closed the door and stepped out into the night air.

The wind continued to blow.

A man they called El Tartamudo came to the Media Luna and asked for Pedro Páramo.

'Why do you want to see him?'

'I want to t-talk with him.'

'He isn't here.'

'T-tell him, when he comes back, that it's about d-don Fulgor.'

'I'll go look for him, but you may have to wait a while.'

'T-tell him it's uh-urgent.'

'I'll tell him.'

El Tartamudo waited, without dismounting from his horse. After a while Pedro Páramo, whom El Tartamudo had never seen, came up and asked:

'What can I do for you?'

'I need to t-talk directly to the *patrón*.'

'I am the *patrón*. What do you want?'

'W-well. Just this. They've m-murdered don Fulgor Sedano. I was w-with him. We'd ridden down to the spillways to find out whuh-why the water had dried up. And wh-while we were doing that a band of m-men came riding toward us. And o-one of them yelled "I n-know him. He's the foreman of the M-Media Luna."

'Th-they ignored me. But they t-told don Fulgor to get off his horse. They s-said they were r-revolutionaries. And th-that they wanted your land. "T-take off!" they told don Fulgor. "R-run tell your *patrón* to be expecting us!" And he st-started off, sc-scared as hell. N-not too fast, because he's so fat; but he ran. They sh-shot him as he ran. He d-d-died with one foot in the air and one on the g-ground.

'I didn't m-move a hair. I waited for n-night, and here I am to t-tell you what happened.'

'Well, what are you hanging around for? Get on your way. Go tell those men that I'm here anytime they want to see me. I'll deal with them. But first ride by La Consagración ranch. You know El Tilcuate? He'll be there. Tell him I need to see him. And tell those men that I'll expect them at the first opportunity. What brand of revolutionaries are they?'

'I don't know. Th-that's what they c-called themselves.'

'Tell El Tilcuate that I need him here *yesterday*.'

'I w-will, *patrón*.'

Pedro Páramo again closed the door to his office. He felt old and weary. He lost no time worrying about Fulgor, who'd been, after all, 'more of the next world than this.' He'd given all he had to give. He could be useful, though no more than any other man. 'But those dumb bastards have never run into a boa constrictor like El Tilcuate,' he thought.

And then his thoughts turned to Susana San Juan, always in her room sleeping, or if not sleeping, pretending to be. He had spent the whole night in her room, standing against the wall and observing her in the wan candlelight: sweaty face, hands fidgeting with the sheets and tugging at her pillow until it was in shreds.

Ever since he had brought her to live with him, every night had been like this, nights spent watching her suffering, her endless agitation. He asked himself how long it would go on.

He hoped not long. Nothing can last forever; there is no memory, however intense, that does not fade.

If only he knew what was tormenting her, what made her toss and turn in her sleeplessness until it seemed she was being torn apart inside.

He had thought he knew her. But even when he found he didn't, wasn't it enough to know that she was the person he loved most on this earth? And – and this was what mattered most – that because of her he would leave this earth illuminated by the image that erased all other memories.

But what world was Susana San Juan living in? That was one of the things Pedro Páramo would never know.

'The warm sand felt so good against my body. My eyes were closed, my arms flung wide and my legs open to the breeze from the sea. The sea there before me, stretching toward the horizon, leaving its foam on my feet as the waves washed in ...'

'Now that's her talking, Juan Preciado. Don't forget to tell me what she says.'

'... It was early morning. The sea rose and fell. It slipped from its foam and raced away in clear green silent waves.

'"I always swim naked in the sea," I told him. And he followed me that first day, naked too, phosphorescent as he walked from the sea. There were no gulls; only those birds they call "sword beaks," that grunt as if they're snoring and disappear once the sun is up. He followed me the first day; he felt lonely, even though I was there.

'"You might just as well be one of the birds," he said. "I like you better at night when we're lying on the same pillow beneath the same sheets in the darkness."

'He went away.

'I went back. I would always go back. The sea bathes my ankles, and retreats; it bathes my knees, my thighs; it puts its gentle arm around my waist, circles my breasts, embraces my throat, presses my shoulders. Then I sink into it, my whole body. I give myself to its pulsing strength, to its gentle possession, holding nothing back.

'"I love to swim in the sea," I told him.

'But he didn't understand.

'And the next morning I was again in the sea, purifying myself. Giving myself to the waves.'

As dusk fell, the men appeared. They were carrying carbines, and cartridge belts crisscrossed their chests. There were about twenty of them. Pedro Páramo invited them in to eat. Without removing their sombreros, or uttering a word, they sat down at the table and waited. The only sounds came as they drank their chocolate and ate repeated servings of tortillas and beans.

Pedro Páramo watched them. These were not faces he knew. El Tilcuate stood right behind him, in the shadows.

'Señores,' said Pedro Páramo, when he saw they were through. 'What else can I do for you?'

'You own all this?' one of them asked with a sweeping gesture.

But another man interrupted:

'I do the talking here!'

'All right. What can I do for you?' Pedro Páramo repeated.

'Like you see, we've taken up arms.'

'And?'

'And nothing. That's it. Isn't that enough?'

'But why have you done it?'

'Well, because others have done the same. Didn't you know? Hang on a little till we get our instructions, and then we'll tell you why. For now, we're just here.'

'I know why,' another said. 'And if you want, I'll tell you. We've rebelled against the government and against people like you because we're tired of putting up with you. Everyone in the government is a crook, and you and your kind are nothing but a bunch of lowdown bandits and slick thieves. And as for the governor himself, I won't say nothing, because what we have to say to him we'll say with bullets.'

'How much do you need for your revolution?' Pedro Páramo asked. 'Maybe I can help you.'

'The señor is talking sense, Perseverancio. You shouldn't let your tongue run on like that. We need to get us a rich man to help outfit us, and who better than this señor here. Casildo, how much do we need?'

'Well, whatever the señor feels he can give us.'

'What! This man wouldn't throw a crumb to a starving man. Now that we're here, we'd ought to grab our chance and take everything he's got, right down to the last scrap of food stuffed in his filthy mouth.'

'Easy now, Perseverancio. You catch more flies with sugar than with vinegar. We can make a deal here. How much, Casildo?'

'Well, I figure off the top of my head that twenty thousand

pesos wouldn't be too bad as a starter. What do the rest of you think? Now, who knows but what our señor here maybe could do a little more, seeing he's so willing to help us. So, let's say fifty thousand. How does that strike you?'

'I'll give you a hundred thousand,' Pedro Páramo told them. 'How many are there of you?'

'I'd say three hundred.'

'All right. I'm going to lend you another three hundred men to beef up your contingent. Within a week you'll have both men and money at your disposal. I'm giving you the money; the men are just a loan. As soon as you're through with them, send them back here. Is that a bargain?'

'You bet.'

'So until a week from now, señores. It's been a pleasure to meet you.'

'All right,' said the last to leave. 'But remember, if you don't live up to your word, you'll hear from Perseverancio, and that's me.'

Pedro Páramo shook the man's hand as he left.

'Which one of them do you think is the leader?' he asked El Tilcuate after they'd gone.

'Well, I think maybe the one in the middle, the one with the big belly who never even looked up. I have a feeling he's the one. I'm not often wrong, don Pedro.'

'You are this time, Damasio. *You're* the leader. Or would you rather not get tied up in this revolution?'

'Well, I have been a little slow getting to it. Considering how much I like a good scrap.'

'You have an idea now what it's all about, so you don't need my advice. Get yourself three hundred men you can trust and sign up with these rebels. Tell them you're bringing the men I promised them. You'll know how to take care of the rest.'

'And what do I tell them about the money? Do I hand that over, too?'

'I'll give you ten pesos for each man. Just enough for their most pressing needs. You tell them I'm keeping the rest here for them. That it isn't a good idea to haul so much money around in times like these. By the way, how would you like that little *rancho* over in Puerta de Piedra? Fine. It's yours, as of this minute. Take this note to my lawyer in Comala, old Gerardo Trujillo, and he'll put the property in your name then and there. How does that sound, Damasio?'

'No need to ask, *patrón*. Though I'd be happy to do this with or without the *rancho* – just for the hell of it. You know me. At any rate, I'm grateful to you. My old woman will have something to keep her busy while I'm off roaring around.'

'And look, while you're at it, round up a few head of cattle. What that *rancho* needs is a little activity.'

'Would you mind if I took Brahmas?'

'Choose any you want, your wife can look after them. Now, to get back to our business. Try not to get too far away from my land, so that when anyone comes they'll find men already here. And come by whenever you can, or when you have news.'

'Be seeing you, *patrón*.'

'What is it she's saying, Juan Preciado?'

'She's saying she used to hide her feet between his legs. Feet icy as cold stones, and that he warmed them, like bread baking in the oven. She says he nibbled her feet, saying they were like golden loaves from the oven. And that she slept cuddled close to him, inside his skin, lost in nothingness as she felt her flesh part like a furrow turned by a plough first burning, then warm and gentle, thrusting against her soft flesh, deeper, deeper, until she cried out. But she says his death hurt her much much more. That's what she said.'

'Whose death does she mean?'

'Must have been someone who died before she did.'

'But who could it have been?'

'I don't know. She says that the night he was late coming home, she felt sure he'd come back very late, maybe about dawn. She thought that because her poor cold feet felt as if they'd been wrapped in something, as if someone had covered them and warmed them. When she woke up she found that her feet were under the newspaper she had been reading while she was waiting for him; although the paper had fallen to the floor when she couldn't stay awake any longer, her feet were wrapped in it when they came to tell her he was dead.'

'The box they buried her in must have split open, because I hear something like boards creaking.'

'Yes, I hear it, too.'

That night she had the dreams again. Why such intense

remembering of so many things? Why not simply his death, instead of this tender music from the past?

'Florencio is dead, señora.'

How big the man was! How tall! And how hard his voice was. Dry as the driest dirt. She couldn't see his body clearly; or had it become blurred in memory? As if rain were falling between them. What was it he had said? Florencio? What Florencio? Mine? Oh, why didn't I weep then and drown myself in tears to wash away my anguish? Oh, God! You are not in Your heaven! I asked You to protect him. To look after him. I asked that of You. But all You care about is souls. And what I want is his body. Naked and hot with love; boiling with desire; stroking my trembling breasts and arms. My transparent body suspended from his. My lustful body held and released by his strength. What shall I do now with my lips without his lips to cover them? What shall become of my poor lips?

While Susana San Juan tossed and turned, Pedro Páramo, standing by the door, watched her and counted the seconds of this long new dream. The oil in the lamp sputtered, and the flame flickered and grew weaker. Soon it would go out.

If only she were suffering pain, and not these relentless, interminable, exhausting dreams, he could find some way to comfort her. Those were Pedro Páramo's thoughts as he stood watching Susana San Juan, following her every movement. What would he do if she died like the flame of the pale light that allowed him to watch her?

He left the room, noiselessly closing the door behind him.

Outside, the cool night air erased Susana San Juan's image from his mind.

Just before dawn, Susana awakened. She was sweating. She threw the heavy covers to the floor, and freed herself of the heat of the sheets. She was naked, cooled by the early morning air. She sighed, and then fell back to sleep.

That was how Father Rentería found her hours later; naked and sleeping.

'Have you heard, don Pedro? They got the best of El Tilcuate.'

'I knew there was shooting last night, because I could hear the racket. But that's all I knew. Who told you this, Gerardo?'

'Some of the wounded made it to Comala. My wife helped bandage them. They said they'd been with Damasio, and that a lot of men died. Seems like they met up with some men who called themselves Villistas.'

'Good God, Gerardo! I see bad times ahead. What do you plan to do?'

'I'm leaving, don Pedro. For Sayula. I'll start over there.'

'You lawyers have the advantage; you can take your fortune with you anywhere, as long as they don't knock you off.'

'Don't you believe it, don Pedro. We have our problems. Besides, it hurts to leave people like you; all your courtesies will be sorely missed. It's fair to say that our world is constantly changing. Where would you like me to leave your papers?'

'Don't leave them. Take them with you. Or won't you be able to look after my affairs where you're going?'

'I appreciate your confidence, don Pedro. Truly I do. Although I venture to say that it won't be possible for me to continue. Certain irregularities ... Let's say ... information no one but you should have. Your papers could be put to bad use if they fell into the wrong hands. The surest thing would be to leave them with you.'

'You're right, Gerardo. Leave them here. I'll burn them. With papers or without them, who's going to argue with me over my property.'

'No one, I'm sure of that, don Pedro. No one. Now I must be going.'

'Go with God, Gerardo.'

'What did you say?'

'I said, may God be with you.'

Gerardo Trujillo, lawyer, left very slowly. He was old, but not so old he had to walk so haltingly, so reluctantly. The truth was that he had expected a reward. He had served don Lucas – might he rest in peace – don Pedro's father; then, and up till now, don Pedro. Even Miguel, don Pedro's son. The truth was that he expected some recognition. A large, and welcome, return for his services. He had told his wife:

'I'm going over to tell don Pedro I'm leaving. I know he'll want to thank me. Let me say that with the money he gives me we can establish ourselves in Sayula and live in comfort for the rest of our days.'

But why is it that women always have doubts? What is it, anyway? Do they receive their information from on high? His wife had not been at all sure he would be rewarded.

'You'll have to work like a dog to keep your head above water. You won't get anything from him.'

'Why do you say that?'

'I just know.'

He was still walking toward the front door, listening for a sudden summons:

'Oh, Gerardo! I've been so preoccupied that I wasn't thinking straight. You know I owe you favours that can't be repaid with money. Here, take this: a small thank-you.'

But the summons never came. He left through the front entrance and untied his horse from the hitching post. He mounted and slowly started back toward Comala, trying not to ride out of earshot, in case anyone called. When he realized that the Media Luna had faded from sight, he thought, 'What a terrible comedown it would be to ask for a loan.'

'Don Pedro. I've come back because I'm not happy with myself. I'd be pleased to continue to look after your affairs.'

He was again sitting in Pedro Páramo's office, which he'd left less than a half hour before.

'Fine with me, Gerardo. Here are the papers, right where you left them.'

'I'd also appreciate ... My expenses ... Moving ... A small advance on my fees ... And a little something extra, if that seems all right.'

'Five hundred?'

'Couldn't we make it a little, well, just a little more?'

'Will a thousand do?'

'How about five?'

'Five what? Five thousand pesos? I don't have that much. You of all people know that everything I have is tied up. Land, cattle. You know that. Take a thousand. That's all you'll need.'

Trujillo sat thinking. With his head on his chest. He heard pesos clinking on the desk where Pedro Páramo was counting the money. He was remembering don Lucas, who had always put off paying his fees. And don Pedro, who'd started with a clean slate. And his son Miguel. What a lot of trouble that boy had caused!

He had got him out of jail at least fifteen times, if not more. And there was the time he'd murdered that man. What was his name? Rentería, yes, that was it. They'd put a pistol in the corpse's hand. Miguelito'd been scared to death, though he'd laughed about it later. How much would just that one time have cost don Pedro if things had moved ahead to legal proceedings? And what about all the rapes, eh? Think of all the times he'd taken money from his own pocket to keep the girls quiet. 'You should be thankful,' he'd told them, 'that you'll be having a fair-skinned baby.'

'Here you are, Gerardo. Take good care of this, because money doesn't grow on trees.'

And Trujillo, who was still deep in his meditations, replied, 'Just like dead men don't spring up from their graves.'

It was a long time till dawn. The sky was filled with fat stars, swollen from the long night. The moon had risen briefly and then slipped out of sight. It was one of those sad moons that no one looks at or pays attention to. It had hung there a while, misshapen, not shedding any light, and then gone to hide behind the hills.

From far away, shrouded in darkness, came the bellowing of bulls.

'Those creatures never sleep,' said Damiana Cisneros. 'They never sleep. They're like the Devil, who's always out looking for souls to spirit away.'

She turned over in bed, putting her face close to the wall. That was when she heard the knocking.

She held her breath and opened her eyes. Again she heard three sharp taps, as if someone were rapping on the wall. Not right beside her, but farther away – although on the same wall.

'Heaven help us! It must have been San Pascual, tapping three times as warning to one of his faithful that his hour has come.'

Since she hadn't made a novena for so long because of her rheumatism, she didn't worry; but she was afraid, and even more than afraid, curious.

She quietly got up from her cot and peered out the window.

The fields were black. Even so, she knew the landscape so well that she could see the large mass of Pedro Páramo's body swinging into the window of young Margarita.

'Oh, that don Pedro!' said Damiana. 'He never gets over chasing the girls. What I don't understand is why he insists on doing things on the sly. If he'd just let me know, I would have told Margarita that the *patrón* had need of her tonight, and he wouldn't have had the bother of leaving his bed.'

She closed the window when she heard the bulls still bellowing. She lay down on her cot and pulled the cover up over her ears, and then lay there thinking about what must be happening to young Margarita.

A little later she had to get up and strip off her nightgown, because the night seemed to have turned hot …

'Damiana!' she heard.

And she was a girl again.

'Open the door, Damiana!'

Her heart had leapt like a toad hopping beneath her ribs.

'But why, *patrón*?'

'Open up, Damiana!'

'But I'm fast asleep, *patrón*.'

Then she had heard don Pedro stalking off down the long corridor, his heels clicking loudly, as they did when he was angry.

The next night, to avoid angering him again, she left the door ajar, and even went to bed naked to make things easy for him. But Pedro Páramo had never returned.

And so tonight, now that she was the head of all the Media Luna servants, and was old and had earned her respect, she still thought of that night when the *patrón* had called, 'Open the door, Damiana!'

And she fell asleep thinking how happy young Margarita must be at this hour.

Later, she again heard knocking, but this time at the main door, as if someone were trying to beat it down with the butt of a gun.

A second time she opened the window and looked out into the night. She saw nothing, although it seemed to her the earth was steaming, as it does after a rain when the earth is roiling with worms. She could sense something rising, something like the heat of many men. She heard frogs croaking, and crickets: a quiet night in the rainy season. Then once again she heard the pounding at the door.

A lamp spilled its light on the faces of a band of men. Then it went out.

'These things have nothing to do with me,' said Damiana Cisneros, and closed her window.

'I heard you got your tail whipped, Damasio. Why did you let that happen?'

'You got the wrong story, *patrón*. Nothing happened to me. I didn't lose a man. I have seven hundred of my own, and a few tagalongs. What happened was that a few of the old-timers got bored with not seeing any action and started firing at a patrol of shave-heads who turned out to be a whole army. Those Villistas, you know.'

'Where had they come from?'

'From the North, levelling everything they found in their path. It seems, as far as we can make out, that they're riding all through here getting the lay of the land. They're powerful. You can't take that from them.'

'Well, why don't you join up with them? I've told you before we have to be on the side of whoever's winning.'

'I've already done it.'

'Then why are you here?'

'We need money, *patrón*. We're tired of eating nothing but meat. We don't have a taste for it anymore. And no one wants to give us credit. That's why we've come, hoping you can buy us provisions and we won't have to steal from anyone. If we were way off somewhere, we wouldn't mind "borrowing" a little from the locals, but everyone around here is a relative, and we'd feel bad robbing them. It's money we need, to buy food, even if only a few tortillas and chillies. We're sick of meat.'

'So now you're making demands on me, Damasio?'

'Oh, no, *patrón*, I'm speaking for the boys. I don't want nothing for myself.'

'It speaks well for you that you're looking after your men, but go somewhere else to get what you need. I've already given you money. Be happy with what you've got. Now I don't want to offer this as advice, but haven't you thought of riding on Contla? Why do you think you're fighting a revolution? Only a dunce would be asking for handouts. You might as well go home and help your wife look after the hens. Go raid some town! You're risking your skin, so why the hell don't others do their part? Contla is crawling with rich men. Take a little out of their hides. Or maybe you think you're their nursemaid and have to look after their interests? No, Damasio. Show them that you're not just out for a good time. Rough them up a little, and the centavos will flow.'

'I'll do like you say, *patrón*. I can always count on good advice from you.'

'Well, make good use of it.'

Pedro Páramo watched as the men rode away. He could hear horses trotting past, invisible in the darkness. Sweat and dust; trembling earth. When the light of fireflies again dotted the sky, he knew all the men had left. Only he remained, alone, like a sturdy tree beginning to rot inside.

He thought of Susana San Juan. He thought of the young girl he had just slept with. Of the small, frightened, trembling body, and the thudding of a heart that seemed about to leap from her chest. 'You sweet little handful,' he had said to her. And embraced her, trying to transform her into Susana San Juan. 'A woman who is not of this world.'

As dawn breaks, the day turns, stopping and starting. The rusty gears of the earth are almost audible: the vibration of this ancient earth overturning darkness.

'Is it true that night is filled with sins, Justina?'

'Yes, Susana.'

'Really true?'

'It must be, Susana.'

'And what do you think life is, Justina, if not sin? Don't you hear? Don't you hear how the earth is creaking?'

'No, Susana, I can't hear anything. My fate is not as grand as yours.'

'You would be frightened. I'm telling you, you would be frightened if you heard what I hear.'

Justina went on cleaning the room. Again and again she passed the rag over the wet floorboards. She cleaned up the water from the shattered vase. She picked up the flowers. She put the broken pieces into the pail.

'How many birds have you killed in your lifetime, Justina?'

'Many, Susana.'

'And you never felt sad?'

'I did, Susana.'

'Then, what are you waiting for to die?'

'I'm waiting for Death, Susana.'

'If that's all, it will come. Don't worry.'

Susana San Juan was sitting propped up against her pillows. Her uneasy eyes searching every comer. Her hands were clasped over her belly like a protective shell. A humming like wings sounded above her head. And the creaking of the pulley in the well. The sounds of people waking up.

'Do you believe in hell, Justina?'

'Yes, Susana. And in heaven, too.'

'I only believe in hell,' Susana said. And closed her eyes.

When Justina left the room, Susana San Juan fell asleep again, while outside the sun sparkled. Justina met Pedro Páramo in the hall.

'How is the señora?'

'Bad,' she replied, ducking her head.

'Is she complaining?'

'No, señor. She doesn't complain about anything; but they say the dead never complain. The señora is lost to us all.'

'Has Father Rentería been to see her?'

'He came last night to hear her confession. She should have taken Communion today but she must not be in a state of grace, because padre Rentería hasn't brought it. He said he'd be here early, but you see the sun's up and he hasn't come. She must not be in a state of grace.'

'Whose grace?'

'God's grace, señor.'

'Don't be silly, Justina.'

'As you say, señor.'

Pedro Páramo opened the door and stood beside it, letting a ray of light fall upon Susana San Juan. He saw eyes pressed tightly shut as if in pain; a moist, half-open mouth; sheets thrown back by insentient hands to reveal the nakedness of a body beginning to twist and turn in convulsions.

He rushed across the brief space separating him from the bed and covered the naked body writhing like a worm in more and more violent contortions. He spoke into her ear, 'Susana!' He repeated, 'Susana!'

The door opened and Father Rentería entered quietly, saying only:

'I've come to give you Communion, my child.'

He waited until Pedro Páramo helped her sit up and arranged her pillows against the headboard. Susana San Juan, still half-asleep, held out her tongue and swallowed the Host. Then she said, 'We had a glorious day, Florencio.' And sank back down into the tomb of her sheets.

'You see that window, doña Fausta, there at the Media Luna where the light is always on?'

'No, Angeles. I don't see any window.'

'That's because the room is dark now. Don't you think that means something bad is going on over there? There's been a light in that window for more than three years, night after night. People who've been there say that's the room of Pedro Páramo's wife, a poor crazy woman who's afraid of the dark. And look, now the light's out. Isn't that a bad sign?'

'Maybe she died. She's been real sick. They say she doesn't know people anymore, and that she talks to herself. It's a fitting punishment for Pedro Páramo, being married to that woman.'

'Poor don Pedro.'

'No, Fausta, he deserves it. That and more.'

'See, the window is still dark.'

'Just let the window be, and let's get home to bed. It's late for two old women like us to be out roaming the streets.'

And the two women, who had left the church about eleven, disappeared beneath the arches of the arcade, watching the shadow of a man crossing the plaza in the direction of the Media Luna.

'Look, doña Fausta. Do you think that man over there is Doctor Valencia?'

'It looks like him, although I'm so blind I wouldn't recognize him if he was right in front of me.'

'But you remember, he always wears those white pants and a black coat. I'll bet something bad is happening out at the Media Luna. Look how fast he's walking, as if he had a real reason to hurry.'

'Which makes me think it really is serious. I feel like I

ought to go by and tell padre Rentería to get out there; that poor woman shouldn't die without confessing.'

'God forbid, Angeles. What a terrible thought. After all she's suffered in this world no one would want her to go without the last rites and then suffer forever in the next life. Although the psychics always say that crazy people don't need to confess, that even if they have sin in their soul, they're innocents. God only knows ... Look! Now the light's back on in the window. I hope everything turns out all right. If someone dies in that house imagine what would happen to all the work we've gone to to decorate the church for Christmas. As important as don Pedro is, our celebration would go right up in smoke.'

'You always think of the worst, doña Fausta. You should do what I do: put everything in the hands of Divine Providence. Say an Ave Maria to the Virgin, and I'm sure nothing will go wrong between now and morning. And then, let God's will be done. After all, she can't be very happy in this life.'

'Believe me, Angeles, I always take comfort from what you say. I can go to sleep with those good thoughts on my mind. They say that our sleeping thoughts go straight to Heaven. I hope mine make it that far. I'll see you tomorrow.'

'Until tomorrow, Fausta.'

The two old women slipped through the half-open doors of their homes. And the silence of the night again fell over the village.

'My mouth is filled with earth.'

'Yes, Father.'

'Don't say, "Yes, Father." Repeat with me the words I am saying.'

'What are you going to say? You want me to confess again? Why again?'

'This isn't a confession, Susana. I've just come to talk with you. To prepare you for death.'

'I'm going to die?'

'Yes, daughter.'

'Then why don't you leave me in peace? I want to rest. Someone must have told you to come keep me awake. To stay with me until sleep is gone forever. Then what can I do to find him? Nothing, Father. Why don't you just go away and leave me alone?'

'I will leave you in peace, Susana. As you repeat the words I tell you, you will drift off, as if you were crooning yourself to sleep. And once you are asleep, no one will wake you ... You will never wake again.'

'All right, Father. I will do what you say.'

Father Rentería, seated on the edge of the bed, his hands on Susana San Juan's shoulders, his mouth almost touching her ear to keep from being overheard, formed each word in a secretive whisper: 'My mouth is filled with earth.' Then he paused. He looked to see whether her lips were moving. He saw her mouthing words, though no sound emerged:

'My mouth is filled with you, with your mouth. Your tightly closed lips, pressing hard, biting into mine ...'

She, too, paused. She looked at Father Rentería from the

corner of her eye; he seemed far away, as if behind a misted glass.

Again she heard his voice, warm in her ear:

'I swallow foamy saliva; I chew clumps of dirt crawling with worms that knot in my throat and push against the roof of my mouth ... My mouth caves in, contorted, lacerated by gnawing, devouring teeth. My nose grows spongy. My eyeballs liquefy. My hair burns in a single bright blaze ...'

He was surprised by Susana San Juan's calm. He wished he could divine her thoughts and see her heart struggling to reject the images he was sowing within her. He looked into her eyes, and she returned his gaze. It seemed as if her twitching lips were forming a slight smile.

'There is more. The vision of God. The soft light of his infinite Heaven. The rejoicing of the cherubim and song of the seraphim. The joy in the eyes of God, which is the last, fleeting vision of those condemned to eternal suffering. Eternal suffering joined to earthly pain. The marrow of our bones becomes like live coals and the blood in our veins threads of fire, inflicting unbelievable agony that never abates, for it is fanned constantly by the wrath of God.'

'He sheltered me in his arms. He gave me love.'

Father Rentería glanced at the figures gathered around them, waiting for the last moment. Pedro Páramo waited by the door, with crossed arms; Doctor Valencia and other men stood beside him. Farther back in the shadows, a small group of women eager to begin the prayer for the dead.

He meant to rise. To anoint the dying woman with the

holy oils and say, 'I have finished.' But no, he hadn't finished yet. He could not administer the sacraments to this woman without knowing the measure of her repentance.

He hesitated. Perhaps she had nothing to repent of. Maybe there was nothing for him to pardon. He bent over her once more and said in a low voice, shaking her by the shoulders:

'You are going into the presence of God. And He is cruel in His judgment of sinners.'

Then he tried once more to speak into her ear, but she shook her head:

'Go away, Father. Don't bother yourself over me. I am at peace, and very sleepy.'

A sob burst forth from one of the women hidden in the shadows.

Susana San Juan seemed to revive for a moment. She sat straight up in bed and said:

'Justina, please go somewhere else if you're going to cry!'

Then she felt as if her head had fallen upon her belly. She tried to lift it, to push aside the belly that was pressing into her eyes and cutting off her breath, but with each effort she sank deeper into the night.

'I ... I saw doña Susanita die.'

'What are you saying, Dorotea?'

'What I just told you.'

Dawn. People were awakened by the pealing of bells. It was the morning of December eighth. A grey morning. Not cold, but grey. The pealing began with the largest bell. The others chimed in. Some thought the bells were ringing for High Mass, and doors began to open wide. Not all the doors opened; some remained closed where the indolent still lay in bed waiting for the bells to advise them that morning had come. But the ringing lasted longer than it should have. And it was not only the bells of the large church, but those in Sangre de Cristo, in Cruz Verde, and the Santuario. Noon came, and the tolling continued. Night fell. And day and night the bells continued, all of them, stronger and louder, until the ringing blended into a deafening lament. People had to shout to hear what they were trying to say. 'What could it be?' they asked each other.

After three days everyone was deaf. It was impossible to talk above the clanging that filled the air. But the bells kept ringing, ringing, some cracked, with a hollow sound like a clay pitcher.

'Doña Susana died.'

'Died? Who?'

'The señora.'

'Your señora?'

'Pedro Páramo's señora.'

People began arriving from other places, drawn by the endless pealing. They came from Contla, as if on a pilgrimage. And even farther. A circus showed up, who knows from where, with a whirligig and a merry-go-round. And musicians. First they came as if they were onlookers, but after a while they settled in and even played concerts. And so, little by little, the event turned into a fiesta. Comala was bustling with people, boisterous and noisy, just like the feast days when it was nearly impossible to move through the village.

The bells fell silent, but the fiesta continued. There was no way to convince people that this was an occasion for mourning. Nor was there any way to get them to leave. Just the opposite, more kept arriving.

The Media Luna was lonely and silent. The servants walked around with bare feet, and spoke in low voices. Susana San Juan was buried, and few people in Comala even realized it. They were having a fair. There were cockfights and music, lotteries, and the howls of drunken men. The light from the village reached as far as the Media Luna, like an aureole in the grey skies. Because those were grey days, melancholy days for the Media Luna. Don Pedro spoke to no one. He never left his room. He swore to wreak vengeance on Comala:

'I will cross my arms and Comala will die of hunger.'

And that was what happened.

El Tilcuate continued to report:

'We're with Carranza now.'

'Fine.'

'Now we're riding with General Obregón.'

'Fine.'

'They've declared peace. We're dismissed.'

'Wait. Don't disband your men. This won't last long.'

'Father Rentería's fighting now. Are we with him or against him?'

'No question. You're on the side of the government.'

'But we're irregulars. They consider us rebels.'

'Then take a rest.'

'As fired up as I am?'

'Do what you want, then.'

'I'm going to back that old priest. I like how they yell. Besides, that way a man can be sure of salvation.'

'I don't care what you do.'

Pedro Páramo was sitting in an old chair beside the main door of the Media Luna a little before the last shadow of night slipped away. He had been there, alone, for about three hours. He didn't sleep anymore. He had forgotten what sleep was, or time. 'We old folks don't sleep much, almost never. We may drowse, but our mind keeps working. That's the only thing I have left to do.' Then he added, aloud: 'It won't be long now. It won't be long.'

And continued: 'You've been gone a long time, Susana. The light is the same now as it was then; not as red, but that same pale light veiled in the white gauze of the mist. Like now. And it was just this hour. I was sitting here by the door, watching it dawn, watching as you went away following the path to Heaven; there, where the sky was beginning to glow with light, leaving me, growing fainter and fainter among the shadows of this earth.

'That was the last time I saw you. As you went by, you brushed the branches of the Paradise tree beside the path, sweeping away its last leaves with your passing. Then you disappeared. I called after you, "Come back, Susana!"'

Pedro Páramo's lips kept moving, whispering words. Then as he pressed his lips together, he opened his eyes, where the pale light of dawn was reflected.

Day was beginning.

At that same hour, doña Inés, the mother of Gamaliel Villalpando, sweeping the street in front of her son's store, saw Abundio Martinez push the half-open door and go inside. He found Gamaliel asleep on the counter, his sombrero over his face as protection against the flies. Abundio waited a while for him to wake up. He waited until doña Inés, who had completed her chore of sweeping the street, came in and poked her son's ribs with the broomstick:

'You have a customer here! Get up!'

Gamaliel sat up, surly and grunting. His eyes were bloodshot from being up so late – and from waiting on drunks – in fact, getting drunk with them. Now, sitting on the counter, he cursed his mother, he cursed himself, and uninterruptedly cursed life, 'which isn't worth shit.' Then he lay back down with his hands stuffed between his legs, and fell asleep still mumbling curses:

'It's not my fault if drunks are still dragging their asses around at this hour.'

'My poor boy. Forgive him, Abundio. The poor man spent the night waiting on some travellers; the more they drank the more quarrelsome they got. What brings you here so early in the morning?'

She was shouting as she spoke, because Abundio was so hard of hearing.

'Well, I need a bottle of liquor.'

'Has Refugio fainted again?'

'No, she died on me, madre Villa. Just last night, about eleven. After I went and sold my burros. I even sold my burros, so I could get help to make her better.'

'I can't hear what you're saying. What did you say? What are you telling me?'

'I said I spent the night sitting up with my dead wife, Refugio. She gave up the ghost last night.'

'I knew I smelled a death. That's what I said to Gamaliel: "I have a feeling that someone's died. I can smell it." But he didn't pay me any mind. Trying to get along with those strangers, the poor man got drunk. You know how he is when he's like that; he thinks everything's funny, and doesn't pay any attention. But, let's see now. Have you invited anyone to the wake?'

'No one, madre Villa. That's why I need the liquor, to ease my sorrow.'

'Do you want it straight?'

'Yes, madre Villa. To get drunk faster. And give it to me quick. I need it right now.'

'I'll give you two for the price of one, because it's you. I want you to tell your poor dead wife that I always thought well of her, and for her to remember me when she gets to the pearly gates.'

'I will, madre Villa.'

'You tell her that before she gets cold.'

'I'll tell her. I know she's counting on you to pray for her.

She died grieving because there wasn't anyone to give her the last rites.'

'What! Didn't you go for padre Rentería?'

'I did. But they told me he was in the hills.'

'What hills?'

'Well, off there somewhere. You know there's a revolution.'

'You mean he's in it, too? God have mercy on our souls, Abundio.'

'What do we care about all that, madre Villa? It doesn't touch us. Pour me another. Sort of on the sly, like. After all, Gamaliel's asleep.'

'Then don't you forget to ask Refugio to pray to God for me; I need all the help I can get.'

'Don't worry. I'll tell her the minute I get home. I'll get her to promise. I'll tell her she has to do it or else you'll be worrying your head about it.'

'That's just what I want you to do. Because you know how women are. You have to see that they do what they promise.'

Abundio Martinez set another twenty centavos on the counter.

'Now I'll take that other one, señora. And if your hand is a little liberal, well, that's up to you. The one thing I promise is that I'll drink this one at home with the departed; there beside my Cuca.'

'Get along then, before my son wakes up. He's pretty sour when he wakes up after a drink. Get on home, and don't forget my message to your wife.'

Abundio left the store sneezing. The liquor was pure

fire, but since he'd been told that drinking it fast made you drunk faster, he gulped down swallow after swallow, fanning his mouth with his shirttail. He meant to go straight home, where Refugio was waiting, but he took a wrong turning and staggered up the street rather than down, following the road out of town.

'Damiana!' called Pedro Páramo. 'Go see who that man is coming down the road.'

Abundio stumbled on, head hanging, at times crawling on all fours. He felt as if the earth were tilting, that it was spinning, and flinging him off. He would make a grab for it, but just when he had a good hold, it would start spinning again … Until he found himself facing a man sitting outside his door.

'I need money to bury my wife,' he said. 'Can you help me?'

Damiana Cisneros prayed: 'Deliver us, O God, from the snares of the Devil.' And she thrust her hands toward Abundio, making the sign of the cross.

Abundio Martinez saw a frightened woman standing before him, making a cross; he shuddered. He was afraid that the Devil might have followed him there, and he looked back, expecting to see Satan in some terrible guise. When he saw nothing, he repeated:

'I've come to ask for a little charity to help bury my wife.'

The sun was as high as his shoulder. A cool, early-morning sun, hazy in the blowing dust.

As if he were hiding from the sunlight, Pedro Páramo's face vanished beneath the shawl covering his shoulders, as Damiana's cries grew louder, cutting through the fields: 'They're murdering don Pedro!'

Abundio Martínez could hear a woman screaming. He didn't know how to make her stop, and he couldn't find the thread of his thoughts. He was sure that the old woman's screams could be heard a long way away. Even his wife must be hearing them, because they were piercing his eardrums, even though he couldn't understand the words. He thought of his wife, laid out on her cot, all alone there in the patio of his house where he had carried her to lie in the cool air, hoping to slow the body from decomposing. His Cuca, who just yesterday had lain with him, live as life, frolicking like a filly, nipping and nuzzling him. The woman who had given him the son who had died almost as soon as he was born, because, they said, she was in such bad health: a sore eye, the ague, a bad stomach, and who knows what all, according to the doctor who'd come at the last minute, after he'd sold his burros to pay for the price of his visit. And none of it had done any good ... His Cuca, lying there in the night dew, her eyes fast shut, unable to see the dawn, this sun ... any sun.

'Help me!' he said. 'I need a little money.'

But he couldn't hear his own words. The woman's screams deafened him.

Small black dots were moving along the road from Comala. Soon the dots turned into men, and then they were standing beside him. Damiana Cisneros had stopped screaming now. She had relaxed her cross. She had fallen to the ground, and her mouth was open as if she were yawning.

The men lifted her from the ground and carried her inside the house.

'Are you all right, *patrón?*' they asked.

Pedro Páramo's head appeared. He nodded.

They disarmed Abundio, who still held the bloody knife in his hand.

'Come with us,' they said. 'A fine mess you've got yourself into.'

He followed them.

Before they got to the village he begged them to excuse him. He walked to the side of the road and vomited something yellow as bile. Streams and streams, as if he had drunk ten litres of water. His head began to burn and his tongue felt thick.

'I'm drunk,' he said.

He returned to where the men were waiting. He put his arms across their shoulders, and they dragged him back, his toes carving a furrow in the dust.

Behind them, still in his chair, Pedro Páramo watched the procession making its way back to the village. As he tried to lift his left hand, it dropped like lead to his knees, but he thought nothing of it. He was used to seeing some part of him die every day. He watched the leaves falling from the Paradise tree. 'They all follow the same road. They all go away.' Then he returned to where his thoughts had been.

'Susana,' he said. He closed his eyes. 'I begged you to come back ...

'An enormous moon was shining over the world. I stared at you till I was nearly blind. At the moonlight pouring over your face. I never grew tired of looking at you, at the vision you were. Soft, caressed by the moonlight, your swollen, moist lips iridescent with stars, your body growing transparent in the night dew. Susana. Susana San Juan.'

He tried to raise his hand to wipe the image clear, but it clung to his legs like a magnet. He tried to lift the other hand, but it slipped slowly down his side until it touched the floor, a crutch supporting his boneless shoulder.

'This is death,' he thought.

The sun was tumbling over things, giving them form once again. The ruined, sterile earth lay before him. Heat scalded his body. His eyes scarcely moved; they leapt from memory to memory, blotting out the present. Suddenly his heart stopped, and it seemed as if time and the breath of life stopped with it.

'So there won't be another night,' he thought.

Because he feared the nights that filled the darkness with phantoms. That locked him in with his ghosts. That was his fear.

'I know that within a few hours Abundio will come with his bloody hands to ask for the help I refused him. But I won't have hands to cover my eyes, to block him out. I will have to hear him, listen until his voice fades with the day, until his voice dies.'

He felt a hand touch his shoulder, and straightened up, hardening himself.

'It's me, don Pedro,' said Damiana. 'Don't you want me to bring you your dinner?'

Pedro Páramo replied:

'I'm coming along. I'm coming.'

He supported himself on Damiana Cisneros's arm and tried to walk. After a few steps he fell; inside, he was begging for help, but no words were audible. He fell to the ground with a thud, and lay there, collapsed like a pile of rocks.

Afterword by Susan Sontag

'I came to Comala because I had been told that my father, a man named Pedro Páramo, lived there. It was my mother who told me. And I had promised her that after she died I would go see him. I squeezed her hands as a sign I would do it. She was near death, and I would have promised her anything.'

With the opening sentences of Juan Rulfo's *Pedro Páramo*, as with the beginnings of Kleist's novella *Michael Kohlhaas* and Joseph Roth's novel *The Radetzky March*, we know we are in the hands of a master storyteller. These sentences, of a bewitching concision and directness that pull the reader into the book, have a burnished, already-told quality, like the beginning of a fairy tale.

But the limpid opening of the book is only its first move. In fact, *Pedro Páramo* is a far more complex narrative than its beginning suggests. The novel's premise – a dead mother sending her son out into the world, a son's quest for his father – mutates into a multi-voiced sojourn in hell. The narrative takes place in two worlds: the Comala of the present, to which Juan Preciado, the 'I' of the first sentences, is journeying; and the Comala of the past, the village of his mother's memories and of Pedro Páramo's youth. The narrative switches back and forth between first person and third person, present and past. (The great stories are not only told in the past tense, they are about the past.) The Comala of the past is a village of the living. The Comala of the present is inhabited only by the dead, and the encounters that Juan Preciado will have when he reaches Comala are with ghosts. Páramo means in Spanish barren plain, wasteland. Not only is the father he seeks dead, but so is everyone else in the village. Being dead, they have nothing to express except their essence.

'In my life there are many silences,' Rulfo once said. 'In my writing, too.'

Rulfo has said that he carried *Pedro Páramo* inside him for many years before he knew how to write it. Rather, he was writing hundreds of pages and then discarding them. He once called the novel an exercise in elimination. 'The practice of writing the short stories disciplined me,' he said, 'and made me see the need to disappear and to leave my characters the freedom to talk at will, which provoked, it would seem, a lack of structure. Yes, there is a structure in *Pedro Páramo*, but it is a structure made of silences, of hanging threads, of cut scenes, where everything occurs in a simultaneous time which is a no-time.'[1]

Pedro Páramo is a legendary book by a writer who became a legend, too, in his lifetime. Rulfo was born in 1918 in a village in the state of Jalisco, came to Mexico City when he was fifteen, studied law at the university, and began writing, but not publishing, in the late 1930s. His first stories appeared in magazines in the 1940s, and a collection of stories came out in 1953. It was called *El llano en llamas*, which has been translated into English under the title *The Burning Plain and Other Stories*.[2]

Pedro Páramo appeared two years later. The two books established him as a voice of unprecedented originality and authority in Mexican literature, and their influence was immediate and vast throughout the entire world of literature written in Spanish. Quiet (or taciturn), courteous, fastidious, learned, and utterly without pretensions, Rulfo was a kind of invisible man – who earned his living in ways entirely unconnected with literature (for years he was a tire salesman), who married and had children, and who spent most nights of his life reading ('I travel in books') and listening to music. He also was extremely famous, and revered by his fellow writers. It is rare for a writer to publish his first books when he is already in his mid-forties, even rarer for first books to be immediately acknowledged as masterpieces. And rarer still for such a writer never to publish another book. A novel called *La Cordillera* was announced as forthcoming by Rulfo's publisher for many years, starting in the late 1960s – and announced by the author as destroyed, a few years before his death in 1986.

Everyone asked Rulfo why he did not publish another book, as if the point of a writer's life is to go on writing and publishing. In fact, the point of a writer's life is to produce a great book – a book which will last – and this is what Rulfo did. No book is worth reading once if it is not worth reading many times. García Márquez has said that after he discovered *Pedro Páramo* (with Kafka's *Metamorphosis*, the most influential reading of his early writing years), he could recite from memory long passages and eventually knew the whole book by heart, so much did he admire it and want to be saturated by it.

Rulfo's novel is not only one of the masterpieces of twentieth-century world literature, but one of the most influential of the century's books; indeed it would be hard to overestimate its impact on literature in Spanish in the last forty years. *Pedro Páramo* is a classic in the truest sense. It is a book that seems, in retrospect, as if it had to be written. It is a book that has profoundly influenced the making of literature and continues to resonate in other books. This new translation, which fulfils the wish Juan Rulfo expressed to me when I met him in Buenos Aires shortly before his death that *Pedro Páramo* appear in an accurate and uncut English translation, is an important literary event.

Notes

1   From a text by Rulfo in *Inframundo: The Mexico of Juan Rulfo* (Mexico City: Ediciones del Norte, 1983). This is the English-language version of a book of photographs by Rulfo, first published by the Instituto de Bellas Artes in Mexico City in 1980.

2   *The Burning Plain and Other Stories*, translated by George D. Schade (Austin: University of Texas Press, 1971).

28904290R00088

Printed in Great Britain
by Amazon